SARAH, HAGAR
AND THEIR
HUSBAND ABRAHAM

To George & Aubrey

Jeanette Fauvie Johnson

SARAH, HAGAR AND THEIR HUSBAND ABRAHAM

Jannetta Faires Johnson

To order additional copies of this book, contact:
Xlibris Corporation
1-888-795-4274
www.Xlibris.com
Orders@Xlibris.com
19032

FOREWARD

Why can't the Jews and Arabs get along? How come, if Jews, Christians and Muslims all claim the patriarch Abraham as an ancestor, we people are so different? Why are there so many religions in the world? This book is not going to answer all those questions but it may well offer a clue as to why we are who we are today and will take us back to the beginning. Or it may turn out that we are pleasantly surprised that we get along in this world with our several-hundred-times-removed cousins as well as we do.

This story is not original. It is taken faithfully from the first book of the Bible. Every thing that is not in the Bible is the fiction part. Perhaps Sarah and Hagar will become real to you, also. Perhaps you will see God's hand in the hard parts of their lives and see that even then, "all things work together for good to them that love God." Romans 8:28

Jannetta Faires Johnson

CHAPTER ONE

Sarah did not know when she first fell in love with her strapping older half-brother. The earliest memory of him was when she was five, though she recalled that no one had to tell her his name. Abraham was already big enough to go sheep shearing with the men of the family when the incident happened. It was nothing but it was everything to Sarah.

Bena, Sarah's mother, was Terah's concubine. But Abraham's mother was a wife. Bena and Sarah had been assigned a tent some eight furlongs from the wife's, at the wife's insistence.

Not a day went by without Bena saying to the child, *"We should not complain for few are treated so respectfully as we nor have such a large tent and food for every meal."* Yet Sarah sensed early that Bena was speaking to Bena, telling herself to accept her lot in life. Sarah often saw her mother gazing wistfully into the distance as though she dwelt in the past or as though she was longing for someone special to come. Sarah asked her one-day if it was Terah that she was wishing to see, only to be told that she had grown up things in her childish mind and the gods would not be pleased.

Terah rarely came to the tent but when he did it was an honor and a time of concealed joy. Later they would laugh that he always smiled at the child and asked, *"Now what do you call her?"*

Bena would tease, *"A father should remember his daughter's name. If you do not know, I shall not tell you."*

Sarah always smiled as she recalled one particular conversation. *"Then I shall ask the child herself."*

"I shall tell you neither," Sarah shot back, prancing past him, her long hair swinging over a cocked shoulder. If he considered her response defiance, he let it pass.

"Then I shall call you Lily for you are as pretty as the flowers that grow in the vale."

For many moons afterwards Sarah ignored her mother when addressed by her birth name. Bena tired of the Sarah/Lily name game and one day placed her hands on the child's shoulder, looked her firmly in the face and said, *"You should have many sisters, and brothers, too, for you insist too much on your own whims. I have not been hard enough. You do not consider others for there has never been a need to do so. You do not even give respect to the mother who bore you and gave you the name Sarah."*

The child drew herself tall, stuck out her chin and replied, *"There is nothing as pretty as a lily. If I should have had many brothers and sisters, why did you not bear them?"*

The question pierced Bena's heart like a shot arrow. She could almost feel the blood seeping from the wound at the same time the tears made their way down her tanned cheeks. Sarah saw the hurt and became quite the contrite one. She sought to comfort her mother, all the time wondering what she said wrong.

Bena grew up dreaming that she would be a wife one day and the mother of many children. Soon after becoming a woman, Bena had a specific husband in her dreams, but her father ended all that one warm spring afternoon. She understood and she did not fault him for feeling he had too many female mouths to feed; though the deed hurt as if it were yesterday.

She was fourteen when her father came home and instructed that she was to wash her face, comb her hair and put on her ragged dress. Quickly she did as she was told and emerged from the tent to find a tall, imposing figure of a man talking with her father.

"Here she is. She is Bena, a virgin of fourteen years and fit as a young doe." Her father took her hand and turned her around so that the stranger could see every angle of her youthful femininity.

Then her father said, *"Bena, this man is Terah. He may consider making you his concubine. He is a Semite who lives near Ur and can well afford to give me many sheep and goats to offset the loss of my favorite daughter. Is she not fair enough to please you, Terah?"*

"She is very fair indeed and any man would desire her. My own need to lie with a woman has lessened over the years, seeing I have a young wife and there is always one task waiting for me before finishing the other."

"Bena," her father said, *"Go call you brothers and sisters."* She excused herself and returned shortly with seven children, ranging down to a baby perched on the hip of a girl younger but the image of Bena. The hollow eyes of the children and their protruding bellies made Terah ask, *"How much for the girl?"*

"Twelve sheep and twelve goats," the man answered, thinking himself brazen to ask so much.

Terah choked on the words. *"Let it be."* Then he instructed, *"On the morrow see that she is ready. I will send my servants with the asking price."* He cast an apologetic look at Bena, turned and never looked back.

The Youth Choir of
Lawrenceville First Baptist Church
presents

Christmas

with (out) Jesus

Music arrangement: Robert Sterling   Drama: Bob Hoose

December 15, 2004
6:30 p.m. – In the Chapel
Dr. G. Lamar Holley – Pastor

"Christmas with (out) Jesus"

Youth Choir

Craig Bland
Abby Crowe
Elizabeth Damon
Josh Damon
Caitlin Gibson
Christy Gibson
Trevor Giese
Elizabeth Harris
Matthew Josey
Bryna Lamb
Katherine Lingenfelter

Leah Lukens
Kelley Mhoon
Ryan Miller
Jacob Plunkett
Bryan Prevatte
Kristen Prevatte
Melissa Sagneri
Addie Shue
Erin Simonton
Laney Stovall
Kristen Tribble

Character Analysis

"Christmas Hoohah"

Sara: A short tempered teen who finds herself hampered by the stupidity of it all.

Jack: Honor student/moderator type who wants to do the best he can within the system.

Kim: Not too bright, but sincere teen who likes parties.

Rodney: Editor-of-the-school-newspaper type who needs to follow the rules.

"Thoughts"

Mick: A guy who is comparing choices that we make today with choices that changed the past.

Larry: A studious individual who likes to think things through.

Sally: A young girl with a challenge for us.

Program

Joy to the World
*Narrators: Erin Simonton, Katherine Lingenfelter,
Ryan Miller, Kristen Prevatte, Elizabeth Damon,
Bryan Prevatte
Soloist: Josh Damon*

Welcome to Our World
*Narrator: Laney Stovall
Soloist: Caitlin Gibson*

Skit: "Christmas Hoohah"
*Sara: Addie Shue   Kim: Melissa Sagneri
Jack: Josh Damon   Rodney: Matthew Josey*

What's Christmas without Jesus
Soloist: Laney Stovall

The Night that Christ Was Born

Monologues: "Thoughts"
*Mick: Craig Bland   Larry: Jacob Plunkett
Sally: Kristen Prevatte*

Not That Far from Bethlehem
Soloist: Bryna Lamb

And It Came to Pass

Director: *Ed Lawrie*
Assistants: *Harry Gibson, Ken Josey*
Sound: *Ben Damon, Randy Harris*

CHAPTER TWO

Ur was pleasant enough but Bena found herself melancholic and full of longings for home. She recognized that it was guilt, not love nor lust that prompted Terah's visits, infrequent though they were. Sometimes when he stopped by he would not know her, as a man knows a woman. The day Bena told him that she was with child was the last day his flesh ever touched hers.

The child gave Bena's life new meaning and perhaps served as Terah's excuse for coming less often. Bena called the child 'Sarah' and marveled daily at her growth and development. In Sarah's fifth summer Terah came to announce that Bena was to move to a larger more accommodating tent. Two days later a servant came to bear her earthly goods to the new abode. It was away from all the other tents, but set near an almond and fig grove and was the finest Bena had ever been inside. Her joy was apparent in simultaneous laughter and tears and her daughter asked over and over again, *"Do we live here?"*

There were nine supporting poles, indicating this was to be permanent location. She counted the poles aloud and the servant said, *"It is just as father Fabal instructed years ago. There is none finer or more sure."*

The flat top was made of black goat hair to repel any rain that might come. The sides could be raised with only a weak tug on a cord. Moreover, the tent had two compartments and there was goatskin carpet down the middle of the first compartment, secured to three of the poles so it would stay in place.

A few weeks after they were settled, Sarah rushed in excitedly, *"Father is coming. I see him."* She ran in his direction while Bena glanced about the tent to see that nothing was out of order. She rehearsed her words of gratitude, but they went unsaid when she saw the agony on his face.

"Keep the child close to the tent. Do no talk to anyone," he admonished.

"Why? "What?" she stammered.

"It's a consumption, a fever. We do not know, but my son Haran and his wife are near to death. One of their children may suffer the same sickness. Pray to the Goddess of Healing on their behalf."

Bena asked guardedly, *"And if my prayers be not heard, shall I serve as a mourner?"*

"It would not be wise," was his reply. Before he left he laid out a plan for her to place a white fabric from the overhang of the black covering of her tent should she or the child be felled by the illness.

Bena said many prayers but less than a week had gone by before she heard great wailing and lamenting. Two days later, the sounds were heard again, this time even louder and longer. Sarah wanted an explanation and Bena could only surmise that first it was the son's wife and then the son. Her conjecture was confirmed a few days afterwards when Terah came to make them aware of the adult's deaths and the progress of the child. Bena offered help when Terah said his wife was burdened with the care of the three orphaned children, Milcah, Ischar and the infant Lot. Her offer was declined.

Bena urged Terah to rest a while and told Sarah to bring her father some bread and a bowl of the goat cheese she had just finished. Terah would have declined had the child not lept so enthusiastically to the task. When he tasted the cheese, he raised an eyebrow, licked his lips, and asked, *"Is it always so savory?"*

Finishing off the last crumb, he said that no one is his household, neither blood kin nor servants, could make such fine cheese and proclaimed Bena the official cheese maker for the clan. Henceforth, there were comings and goings as milk was delivered regularly and exchanged for the cheese. Bena never dreamed that goat cheese would change her life but that is the way it turned out. Children accompanied adults and for the first time in all her years Sarah could interact with humans her age. A lad accompanied his servant father the day the large jar full of milk was brought. Sarah wondered how the jar could be so big and was spellbound at the boy's account of watching the bottle being made. He told her of how the fat he-goat was slaughtered and his feet and head cut off and insides removed through the neck opening. Sarah listened wide-eyed to the tale of tanning the hide just so the milk could be brought for her mother to make the cheese. She then fell to bemoaning the death of the he-goat, but the boy assured her that not many he-goats were needed to perpetuate the flock.

Perhaps the fact that others were seen about the tent was why Abraham (his kin called him Abram) wandered that direction when he and Sarah had that first encounter.

Or perhaps it was his state of mind. Or perhaps he was in no hurry to get home since without fail he would have to explain his return and was sure to face considerable ridicule.

Abraham had been begging his father to go spring sheep shearing but Terah would not say yeah nor nay. As the gear was being packed and foodstuff stored in the cart, Abraham became a part of the bustle, meantime, questioning his father with his big imploring eyes.

*"I don't know, son, "*Terah said, as though the risks were being weighed in his mind.

Terah never really instructed him not to go and so Abraham set out with the men. He was large enough and strong enough to wrestle down and hold a sheep but he was hardly more than a child. Abraham observed the men carefully and in his mind was sure he could shear a sheep just as they did. Finally Terah selected a lamb and nodded to Abraham that this one was his. He had no trouble getting the lamb tied down but as he was ready to snip the first handful of wood the lamb flinched. There was a pitiful bleat from the animal and stark fear on the face of the lad. Abraham rose slowly with a handful of bloodstained white wool to meet the stare of his father. *"I knew it was a mistake to let you come. You are but a child. Get home to your mother."* There was no anger in Terah's words, only a self-directed admonition that he should not rush the lad into manhood.

Abraham walked away shaken, with the wool in his cupped hand. He did not go straight home, a four-hour distance had he gone directly and with haste. He wanted to time his arrival so as to reach home just after sunset. There would be fewer questions that way. He also wondered why he was carrying the wool and what he would do with it, but somehow he could not bring himself to discard it in the sand.

Suddenly Abraham realized that he was near the tent of

his father's concubine. He was surprised to hear a childish voice address him. *"I know you. You are Abraham. My name is Sarah. What is that in your hands?"*

Before he could make any response the lass had approached him and was peering at the wool. *"Why do you carry it such a way? It is as though you carry water in your bare hands and trying not to spill a drop. What made the stain?"*

Abraham was embarrassed that he could not prevent his eyes from filling with tears and in his mind he heard his father say again, *"You are but a child,"* and recognized his father spoke the truth. Aloud he answered the girl-child's question, *"The blood of the lamb."*

"How come the blood was spilt?" Sarah questioned.

"I pierced his side. I'm a child. I'm not big enough to go sheep-shearing."

Sarah looked up into his eyes and said, *"I think you are big and think when the lamb becomes a ram next year you should apologize as you shear him. What are you going to do with the wool?"*

"That I am not sure," he responded. *"It's of no value. The birds might use it to make nests but nests are already complete."*

"It should be saved for the next generation. You can show your firstborn the results of his father's first sheep shearing. I am saving my baby sandals for my first daughter."

"You speak beyond your years," he said to her. *"But my mother would never allow bloodstains in the tent and we are too crowded with what my mother would call clutter."*

Sarah hastened, *"My mother will let me do anything I want. She will let me keep it for you."*

"All right. It's a gift until my firstborn comes and then you shall give it back."

Sarah extended her hands and the deal was sealed. She

took the wool as gently as he had held it, as though it were some breathing thing. He looked at her but said nothing before scampering out of sight, his spirits considerably lightened. Sarah busied her mind with what to tell her mother about the wool and where to preserve it. She wanted to find her answers before she faced her mother and she wanted her heart to stop racing. Sarah thought that the wool was the first gift she had ever received, save from her mother. But it was more than a gift; it was a shared trust. She would keep it for him against that day he became a father. She decided it could repose underneath her sleeping mat. There could be no bad dreams that way!

During the following days Sarah replayed the incident with Abraham often in her mind and she was sure that she would be seeing him again soon. But not so. It was the following spring that he appeared without forewarning. He approached with an arm full of wool on a day when the side of the tent was down in the direction from whence he came. Bena saw him first and asked his name, though she had a strong suspicion because of the resemblance to his father. To herself she said, *"Had I a son, this is how he would look!"* To him she said, *"You honor us with your presence."*

By then Sarah had emerged and taken over the conversation, slowly leading him away from her mother's range of hearing.

"I brought you some wool," he told her, *"and it may have been from the same ram. I wasn't sure, so to each one I sheared I whispered, 'if I hurt you last shearing, please forgive me.' See, this wool is pure. I thought you might want some so you could learn to spin."*

"Thank you," Sarah replied, taking the wool, *"but I am going to have many servants when I am big and they will do the spinning. I am going to be a wife."*

"Wives spin. My wife is going to cook and spin and clean. You have grown taller."

"And you have gown man-like. No taller but stronger," she observed with approval, "And I have kept your wool. Is this to be kept with the other?"

"No," he replied, "This is a gift. Perhaps I shall bring you an armload of wool every spring."

"The other wool is under my sleeping mat, but this I shall use to make a pillow for my head."

He changed the subject with, "My father is going to sacrifice a spring lamb to the God Yahweh. He says that long ago our ancestors worshipped Yahweh but then we forgot him because we were few and those around us worshipped all the other gods. We did what we saw others doing."

Sarah thought it strange to have a new god. "My favorite is Ningol because the moon goddess has to be the best god of all. But I could never not pray to Ningol for it is she who makes the seasons come in their order and without her the world would die."

Abraham went on, "But the God Yahweh used to be the God of our ancestors and Father has been praying to him and trying to remember things about him. At one time Yahweh got angry and drowned all the people in the world. Well, he did spare one family. Yahweh is very powerful. Father is descended from one of the sons in the family he spared. He believes his name was Shem, but he is not sure. He has set himself to thinking about where he came from. He knows his father was Nahor."

"Nahor? Shem?" mused Sarah. "If they are your ancestors from your father, then they are my ancestors, too."

"I do not think of you as a little sister so I shall not think of you as having the same ancestors," he told her, "I saw the concubine today for the first time and while I do not like her she is nice and very pretty. You look like her."

"So I am pretty," Sarah twisted his words.

"You are vain and vanity never becomes a woman," he retorted.

CHAPTER THREE

Sarah and Bena saw the smoke rising skyward. They smelled the delicate aroma of burning poplar wood and searing meat on the morning of the first day of the new moon. The faint sound of distant voices could be heard at intervals, saying words in unison. Bena wondered if there was a celebration but Sarah, recalling Abraham's conversation said, *"Father has a new God. He is burning a lamb for him."*

"Who ever heard of such nonsense?" Bena said, shaking her head.

Sarah told her mother all Abraham had said, only to have Bena dismiss it with a *"Well my people never heard of any such god."*

Several weeks later Abraham appeared at the tent and Sarah almost immediately asked about burning the lamb.

"It's a sacrifice," he corrected. *"It was to thank Yahweh for His blessings and it was also for special favor on the failing strength of my mother. She is not strong any more. The work she did is being done by Milcah and even I have to do tasks*

that belong to a woman. Perhaps all that is why the sacrifice had such meaning to me."

Sarah was carefully absorbing every word. She wanted to tease him about being a good husband if he could do woman's work, but it would have been out of keeping with his countenance. Instead she asked him to tell her everything about the sacrifice.

The sweet savor went heavenward in the smoke. Heaven is where Yahweh lives. Father raised his hands upward and talked to his God just as we do other gods. As he made his petitions, he would pause and all of us would say, 'So be it.' I got it wrong the first time and said, 'Let it be,' but I think that was all right. I believe Yahweh heard me anyway. Father says Yahweh is willing to forgive when we do wrong if we sacrifice and are truly regretful.

As if all this were not news enough, Abraham said there was to be a marriage. His brother Nahor was to be united with his niece, Milcah. Terah proposed the union, and both were agreeable, for he did not wish either to marry foreigners who did not believe in the God Yahweh.

"Ur is full of marriageable ones who are strangers and have strange ways," Abraham went on. Then he asked Sarah whether she had ever been inside the city wall. She shook her head no and Abraham told her that she dwelt near Ur but not in Ur. For the first time she learned that they lived in Chaldaea, which was made up of many important cities. Chaldaea, in turn, was a division in the mighty nation of Babylon. The city of Ur, according to Abraham, was getting so many people that the city wall was to be extended almost in sight of their tents. *"I have been inside the city gate with my father,"* he said, *"and some day I shall go as far as the mighty Tigarus and Euphrates Rivers. It is the rivers that make our land produce grass for the animals and fruits and grains. And Yahweh helps, too."* He added as an afterthought.

"Do you not give credit to Ningal the moon goddess?" asked Sarah, incredulously.

"Father thinks Yahweh is the real God."

"Father is wrong," she defied.

"We shall speak of this matter no more today. The servants are overworked. I was sent to get the goat cheese."

Nothing that he could have said would have pleased Sarah more. She immediately brightened with the idea that if he came for the cheese today he would do so in the future and she would see him twice each week. Joy. Joy.

Abraham did come periodically and once brought the child Lot. He explained this by saying Lot wanted for attention and he himself was doing double-duty—getting the goat cheese and getting Lot from underfoot of those who had tasks to perform.

Sarah always made an effort to inquire as to the condition of Abraham's mother. She thought she should feel guilty for doing so, though she did not, since her interest centered primarily on whether her own mother's role would be different once the wife was gone. The report from him was always the same, *"No stronger; perhaps a little weaker."*

Then there was the account of the marriage between Nahor and Milcah and Sarah was disappointed there was little revelry. The wedding supper, Abraham reported, was scarcely more than an ordinary meal. Sarah gathered it was just a matter of pitching a new tent and the couple entering at sunset for their first night together. He added, *"We knew she was a virgin so the wedding bed was not even placed."*

Sarah was not sure she understood the 'wedding bed,' but did not ask. Instead she said, *"I am going to have many people at my wedding supper and fruit and wine and singing. It will be a famous wedding."*

"Many people? You know few. You are a day dreamer of the worst kind."

"Perhaps my husband will know many friends and he will have many family members. I might even let servants be guests when they are not being servants," she retorted.

Abraham looked at the child, maturing but still a child, and asked, *"Do you know that I am old enough to take a wife any day?"*

Sarah suddenly felt chilled, but hiding her grief at his remark, she informed him, *"And I will be old enough in two, three years."*

He infuriated her with, *"Perhaps I shall be tired of my first wife by then and I shall take you as a second wife."*

She did not intend it; in fact, she could hardly believe she did it; but in a flash she scooped up a handful of sand and threw it directly in his face. Undone, she began apologizing and still by impulse began wiping the sand from his stinging, tearing eyes. Her touch must have diffused the anger for he said nothing for a long minute, and then flatly, *"May the God help the man who has you to wife."*

Sarah longed to see Abraham for the next several months and she took to roaming far from the tent, both towards the city of Ur and towards her father's place. Bena warned her of risks, but Sarah could see none. Neither did she see Abraham. She came to know three girls her own age who were often outside the city gathering cooking fire sticks, searching for wild fruits or looking for lign aloes for perfumery.

One day she saw the child Lot and for the first time his brother, Ischar. They gave her no information regarding Abraham, despite subtle inquiries about the well being of other family members.

Some months later, Sarah ventured towards her father's tents when she heard the cries of mourning and saw much coming and going. She encountered a servant who told her that the mistress had died. Bena, at Sarah's insistence and with her help, prepared goat cheese, bread with a jar of honey and a fig cake, which Sarah delivered to the tent of her father. The women were preparing the body for burial in the main tent so that Sarah saw only the men who were outside. She thought her father looked old and she thought Abraham looked the part of a god. Her offering was accepted graciously but only the fewest words were spoken. She left feeling the despondence which they projected, but for a different reason.

Months had elapsed before there was any contact with the father's household. When the day came that they saw Terah approaching their tent, both Sarah and Bena wondered what it meant. Sarah dared hope he was coming to ask her mother to be his new wife, but Bena knew that was highly unlikely. When he left, Sarah still wondered why he came but Bena surmised that he had a restlessness—that was all. This time he did not ask Sarah's name but inquired of Bena, *"She is a child of how many years?"* His comment then was that she looked to be fourteen, not twelve, and that he hoped Bena was teaching her to be industrious and how to prepare delectable food, especially goat cheese.

As Sarah developed physically, so did her longing for Abraham. Some days the pain of first love left her with no appetite for food, talk, nor activity. Other days were buoyed by sight of him from a distance and she had the energy to fly. Her roaming brought her to the attention of two young men from Ur, who heard of her from their sisters. Bena screamed at her, for the first time ever, when she learned from Sarah that she had talked to total strangers in the plain. *"I am going to tell Abraham that they said there was no maid in all Ur as fair as I,"* was her only response.

Before she had the opportunity to do so, Abraham came one evening at sunset, greeting her with, *"I am told that the boys in Ur are saying you are fairer than any of the Chaldaen maidens. Is this true?"*

Sarah dropped her head, looked through her long lashes and said, *"How would I know how fair the Chaldaean girls are? I have only seen three."*

"Woman, stop disquieting me! I do not want you in the company of the men of Ur."

"Why?" was her simple inquiry.

"You know why. You know very well why. Tell me you know why!"

Sarah was outwardly composed and very beautiful as she gazed into his eyes and said, *"I want you to tell me why."*

He looked intently at her and mumbled so softly she was not sure she heard aright, *"Because I love you. I have thought of you days when I have been in the fields alone, nights when I have been under the stars with the sheep, and I cannot bear someone else wanting you."* He gently took her hand into his massive one and tenderly held it to his lips. He longed to enfold her in his arms but knew he best leave that need unfulfilled.

A few days forward a servant told Bena when he came for the goat cheese that Terah and Abraham wished to call that evening. Nothing more of the purpose but surely it dealt with matters of importance. Both women and their tent presented their best appearances when the men arrived. Terah lost no time getting to the purpose of their coming. He advised Bena that Abraham had professed his wish for Sarah to become his wife. Terah was asking Bena for Sarah's hand in marriage with his son.

"She has loved him since she was five," was Bena's reply, *"and some days she is totally love sick. But she is too young. It will be necessary to wait until she is fourteen years."*

"Thirteen," said Sarah as though she had some say in the matter.

A year is a long time to a waiting pair in love. Abraham reminded Terah on the fourteenth day of the month of Abib that he had become a man of twenty-two years and he asked that in recognition of the day he be released from his usual tasks at mid-afternoon so that he could spend part of the afternoon and evening with Sarah. If they were to wed when she became fourteen, he reasoned to his father, she should become accustomed to him and learn what would be expected of her as a wife. Surprisingly, Terah agreed and went on to suggest the fourteenth of each of the next ten months be spent thusly.

And so Abraham shared a simple evening meal with Bena and Sarah. Each time he saw her she seemed more beautiful and more eager to become his wife. They had long talks at sundown and until the stars seemed as numerous as the grains of sand under their feet.

Terah accompanied Abraham on one of these visits, refusing, however, to sup with them. Terah came to talk of his rekindled belief in the God Yahweh. It was easy enough to accept his belief in a new god but irrational that he had decided all the other gods were not gods at all. Bena did not say so, but she thought he spoke like a madman. He was actually believing that his new god was giving him direct messages, which even Sarah knew was not possible. Abraham disagreed none with his father and Sarah told herself that he was humoring his father because of Terah's advancing years. The startling statement from Terah was that he expected his household to follow his example and leadership and give up all gods but the real one. He did exempt Bena but let Sarah know what he expected once Abraham had her to wife.

Sarah preferred talking of the wedding supper rather than who was God but Abraham seemed to be of the same mind as his father. She felt nothing could warp the joy she was experiencing in anticipation of being Abraham's wife.

A few weeks before the marriage date, Terah and Abraham came to the tent with an idea that was a quantity disheartening and a bit exciting. Terah had 'a feeling' that the God Yahweh wished him to leave his lifetime home and travel to some as yet undisclosed destination. He proposed that Abraham and Sarah accompany him and revealed that he was also planning to take the grandson Lot. He went on to let Bena know that his son Nahor and wife Milcah had agreed to befriend her and take care of any needs. Life would go on unchanged except that Nahor would become head of the family that remained. Bena was afraid to say anything lest she be racked with the sobs that were about to surface. She feared disagreeing with a god, for Abraham had said that Yahweh God had destroyed most of the human race years ago and surely the god would drown her too. Losing her daughter to Abraham's nearby tent was grief enough but the very thought of not even knowing where she dwelt was more grievous that death.

The date of departure did not seem as important to Terah as the commitment to go. He thought that well after the wedding would be a pleasing time to Yahweh for the journey to begin.

The wedding supper was all Sarah could have wished. Bena had woven the bride's outer garment of the whitest and finest linen with a thread of gold about the bottom. She and Abraham sat at the honor table neath the shade of a chestnut tree, before many guests, including townspeople Sara had never seen. Sarah had insisted that both a calf and a roebuck be slaughtered for the supper and hearty appetites confirmed that she was right in asking for much meat. Lentils, beans, leeks and great mounds of fruit were consumed in abundance. There was a large raisin cake and several smaller ones located at various tables, making the outdoors smell, in Sarah's words, 'like a wedding festival should.'

Abraham thought the wedding bed was unnecessary but Sarah insisted and Bena prepared it. While Abraham asserted that he was sure of her virginity, Sarah teasingly told him she was allowing no excuse for divorce. And so it was at the conclusion of the supper, Bena led Sarah, and Terah accompanied Abraham to the newly set up small tent where the marriage was consummated. The pure white sheet was carefully laid to catch the bright red drops of blood from Sarah's private parts, caused by that consummation. On the morrow Bena would collect the sheet and the other women would witness that the sheet was taken from the wedding bed and it would be carefully put away in the event of allegations in the future.

The dreaded word from Terah came only a few days after the marriage. He was becoming restless and more consumed with his God's command to follow Him to a new home. It was Sarah's dream to present Bena with a grandson before any departure, but Terah's orders from his God were taking on urgency. Daily the plan took shape. Sarah, being the only woman, would be allowed to select whatever food stuffs she wished to take, cooking and cleaning utensils, medicinal supplies and feminine needs. The men would carry as few personal items as possible and would build two new carts and a sled to transport two tents, clothing and necessities. They would set out with twenty goats, thirty sheep, one male and two female calves, three donkeys and a pair of peafowls. Terah emphatically ordered no idols, nor so much as a reminder of a heathen god, be taken.

Nahor and Milcah visited Bena and welcomed her graciously into the warmth of the family. Also, it was planned that her tent be re-pitched near theirs. Since Sarah was with Abraham near the main tent, but frequently at the tent that had been her home, it was easy for Bena to accept a place as a part of the non-nomadic remaining group.

The new carts and sled were assembled and items to be packed laid aside. The bittersweet time came to depart and everyone had warnings, blessings, good wishes and physical farewells for every one else. Lot was outwardly unemotional since he told himself that he was too big to cry and that he would be driving one of the donkeys.

Sarah wept as she hugged her mother and kissed her cheek many times. Her only words were, *"Mother, I will never see you again, but I must go. I am a wife, you know!"*

And so they departed to only God knew where. Terah sensed the leading to go north and in that direction they headed. Travel was slow for many reasons, one being that Terah spent hours under the stars or in the freshness of morning communing with his God. Sarah found it difficult to do all the tasks expected but she enjoyed being the only female, a first time for her. In addition to the passion of being newly wed, she enjoyed getting to know her father/father-in-law as a person. Lot respected her authority and sprang to assist in any possible chore, also a new experience.

Soon the terrain was different and Sarah saw trees and rock formations that were new to her. Sometimes they met caravans of traders and a goat would be exchanged for fresh foods, eggs and once a bracelet for Sarah. At other times they met shepherds leading their flock to pasture and exchanged news of where the most fertile land lay and where wild animals or thieves lurked. In response to the question of their destination, Terah's answer was always, *"We follow the God Yehweh, also called Jehovah, to the place He leads us,"* which was usually considered a non-answer. They found no one else familiar with Terah's God.

Sarah talked with Abraham of her fear, and at the same time desire, to have a child. She worried as to who would assist in the birthing and whether she could maintain her tasks and travel routine. Abraham seemed not that concerned and responded, *"We will leave that to Yahweh. He will see that a child is conceived or not conceived."*

"I thought you were in charge of that," she snapped.

He pulled her backwards into his arms, leaning her head on his chest and said, *"Sarah, you do not trust our God as I do. He is with us here in this place and now in this place and as long as we please him, He is going to take care of us. Can you accept that and not fret about something that may happen out in the future?"*

"My husband, you sound just like your father," she said as she smiled up at him.

Sarah lost count of time but they had traveled at least eight months. Abraham could both read and write and he chronicled some events of the journey and kept a record of days as they elapsed. Sarah was careful not to ask how long they had traveled for fear he would take it as complaining. And she was careful not to voice concern for her mother. Her primary unasked question, however was, *"If we do not know where we are going, how are we going to know when we get there?"*

Abraham estimated that they had traveled most six hundred miles when they came to a place where edifices had been erected on both sides of the roadway to signify that they were entering a new nation. Abraham looked at the markings on the rocks and exclaimed, *"We have come to the Land of Canaan."* The roadway widened and was more than the well-worn paths they had been traveling. So many journeyed the road that it was necessary to drive the animals along side the highway so as not to incur the wrath of impatient travelers. Most seemed in haste and did not stop to pass the time of day with Abraham or his father. One aging traveler, pulling a cart, paused to inquire whether they wished to purchase a fine shawl for the beautiful lady. The opportunity was declined but Terah engaged him in questions about the land. They learned that the same quality roadway would lead them to Babylon, Assyria or Egypt. The stranger pointed towards the Lebanon Mountains and in the opposite direction, the Great Sea Border. They could travel one hundred fifty miles due north and still be in Canaan. The man told Terah where fertile, well-watered valleys could be found and wished him good fortune.

There were shepherds to be seen, for feeding land was plentiful. The animals had grazed little as they had been driven onward for months and they attacked the verdant grass from sun up to sun down, soon becoming fat and many of the females began the process of reproducing. Sarah was able to wash family garments in a stream near their camp and for herself she would have been willing to call this idyllic spot home.

The peafowl hens started laying eggs again but Terah said to the larger one as she dropped an egg in a secluded clump of grass, *"No need trying to nest here. You will have to wait until we move on to the city of Haran."* Sarah shook her head, wishing that she had been afforded the same courtesy of being told that they were to move on and smiled that she had to get her information from a peafowl.

One of the men always stayed nearby while the others took turns venturing off to explore the countryside and talk to the settlers. It was indeed a land flowing with milk and honey and they frequently brought home fruits or foodstuff gathered from the wilds. This was why Sarah regretted Terah's announcement that the following day they were to move towards the city-kingdom of Haran.

By dawn the next morning they had finished their bread and milk and had begun packing and tying goods onto the carts, penning the fowl and coaxing animals that wanted to graze to move on instead. The trek to Haran took many weeks because they moved only in the cool of the mornings, leaving the afternoons for feeding and resting. They frequently inquired the direction and distance to Haran of travelers they met. As they neared the city, Abraham and Lot went to scout the land and find the best spot in which to settle.

One afternoon while they were away, Sarah had an opportunity to have a serious talk with Terah after he had awakened from an afternoon sleep. *"Father,"* she said, *"what do you seek? What does Yahweh want of us?"*

Terah took note of her use of the "us," for usually she referred to Yahweh as "your God." *"Daughter,"* he answered, *"what we seek is still partly behind a veil, which may or may not be lifted in the near days to come. I search to discover whether there are large groups of people who believe in the one true God. If I find no such people, then I shall seek to establish such a nation, perhaps. Perhaps."*

"We best find a people then, for we are not likely to build a nation seeing you are old. Lot has no wife because he is still young, and I am barren after two full years of marriage. Is it not laughable that we should found a nation?"

Terah chuckled with her but said, *"If Yahweh wishes us to become a nation, we will become a nation. Always remember that with him nothing is impossible."*

Soon the place to settle had been decided on and the unpacking process began one more time. The new spot was well pleasing to Sarah; in fact, she could think of nothing it lacked. The tents were pitched near a stream bringing cool water from the mountains, underneath a grove of fig trees and within sight of hazel trees clustered with nuts soon ready for gathering. There were townspeople living within two hours walking distance and merchants passed to and fro on the highway almost within sight of their camp. The men busied themselves with the increase in their flocks, trading with the traveling merchants and getting acquainted with the leading men of the city. Abraham found skin writing tablets and brick engraved with lettering in a shop that sold no other kinds of merchandise. He found the men of the town well informed, not only of the past events, but events of the present as well. He came to talk with a man who told him that his own wife had not conceived a child and soon the man and Abraham had made plans for their families to meet. Thus began the getting acquainted with both men and women of Haran and thus the door was opened for Lot to come to know persons, especially females, of his own age.

Life was good and they lacked nothing—nothing save a son of the next generation. Sarah knew there was plenty of time and told herself that her body had hardly reached full maturity. Terah remained near the camp more and more and it was Abraham whom the townspeople saw as the head of the family. True, it was he whose business skills began to bring the family wealth. At his invitation, Sarah visited the merchants with him and selected jewelry and fashions of the day. Too, they engaged day servants and herdsmen to aid in the ever-growing required number of tasks.

One day Sarah's ear caught the beautiful musical tones coming from a maid who had been employed to assist with household chores. She listened more carefully; charmed by the singing, stunned by the song. The words extolled the mating of the god Baal with the goddess Ashtoreth, exaggerating the copulating anatomy of each. A shocked Sarah expressed her revulsion, only to hear the response, *"Oh, it is a hymn of our worship to the sun god and goddess. All young maidens serve as princesses at our festivals and I am pleased to say that many honorable men of the city come to my stall during the worship. A few men prefer not the pleasure of women but of other men instead. At the last festival we had three stalls for those so inclined. Our festivals are joyous*

*and people come from across the land. Perhaps you would like
to serve as a princess; you are fair and many men would wish
to worship with you."*

Sarah almost screamed, *"Baal and Ashteroth are not gods
and what you speak of is not the way to worship. There is but
one God and He is not to be worshipped in such a vile way.
Do not sing that song in my presence henceforth."*

The maiden spoke in surprise, *"You are a stranger and
you do have strange ways."*

As soon as Abraham came home Sarah told him what the
maid had said, only to find that it was no surprise to him. He
had learned from the townspeople of their misguided worship
practices and added that this was why he did not allow Sarah
to go into the town alone. He wished her neither to hear of
this nor to be desired by men she might meet.

Afterwards Sarah thought less and less of the Canaanites
and had more and more respect for the one God. She
wondered why Yahweh did not punish such wrongdoings
by sending another flood. Later when the spring rains were
late, she wondered if perhaps Yahweh had decided to use a
drought instead of a flood. But then Terah became ill and
she wondered if they were being punished instead of the
Canaanites. Soon Terah was unable to raise himself from
his mat and a servant was taken to attend him at all times,
in addition to the constant presence of at least one of his
family. Abraham said prayers aloud and Sarah said silent
prayers in his behalf. Finally Abraham told Sarah that they
must begin to think of his burial, for each day brought him
closer to death. At sundown Abraham and Sarah walked
hand in hand, hardly talking, as they selected a gravesite. An
appropriate spot was found under a mighty oak tree and as
they stood there Sarah slipped her arms around Abraham
and between sobs extracted a promise that she be buried by
his side, not alone in a strange field.

The brook was beginning to slow to a trickle and Lot went to the mountain to find cool water to bathe Terah's brow and moisten his lips those last few days. He departed his life at a sunrise and his son and grandson cleansed the body and put on the spiced grave clothes, while the servants opened the grave in preparation of the burial at sundown. Some of the townspeople came and while Abraham graciously accepted their condolences he said the burial ritual would be a family one.

Later that night Lot asked if it would be acceptable if he brought his sleeping mat to their tent, not ready to be alone yet.

Soon after Terah was released from life, Abraham told Sarah that Yahweh had given him a definite impression that he should take up the call that first came to his father Terah in the land of Ur and that he should get to a place, which he would be shown for a special purpose. He added, *"Sarah, our God will make of us a great nation if we do as he says. He has told me that. He has also said that we can help other people as we are helped by him."*

"Then by all means we must follow where He leads. Though, I doubt we will find any land that could please us more than here," was her response to her husband's implied wish to follow his God. Lot had to be brought in on the idea of moving again, an idea he did not embrace warmly.

This move, after many years of being settled, was of larger magnitude than others. There were now many animals requiring provender, for the growing season was at an end, more raiment and more cooking utensils. Abraham told the herdsmen of his plan and offered a pleasing reward to any who wished to continue in his employ. Some of the men had families and Abraham agreed these additional souls could travel with them. By the time they departed a month hence, it appeared that an entire nation was migrating.

They traveled half the length of the land of Canaan, again moving only a few miles each day. Sarah enjoyed the companionship of the other women and especially the children. Most of the shepherds' wives hired on as household servants. The women twittered about where they would settle and were overjoyed that Abraham halted when they reached Shechem. They stopped in a lush valley between Mount Ebol and Mount Gerizim, and made haste to pitch their tents on the outskirts of the city. Abraham built an altar to God and sacrificed a lamb as an act of worship and gratitude. He made sure all the souls with him, save those duty exempted, were present for the worship.

But Abraham was not at peace. After only a few months he gave the word that they would be traveling southward on the day following the morrow. This move was difficult for hearts were not in the leaving, despite the fact that they traveled less than twenty miles. Much of the land was settled and they found it necessary to move among the hills and mountain slopes in order to have sufficient land space. They came to Bethel and Abraham gave word that the mountain before them was "it." Though it was not as desirable as places they had left, it did afford a panoramic view of Bethel and other parts of Canaan. While everyone else was busy unloading and setting up, Abraham was busy building an altar.

CHAPTER FOUR

Abraham spent much time in thinking. Frequently he told Sarah his thoughts and plans, but at other times he did not. Sometimes he talked to the servants, or anyone who would listen, of the one God Yahweh. Abraham told only Sarah that God had said He would give all the land their feet had touched in Canaan to their heirs. Sarah did not doubt but wondered how such would be possible since the Canaanites in the land were many.

She did begin to have doubts as consecutive dry seasons came upon them and the animals grew thin and spent their days in pitiful bleatings as they picked over the dry scrub grass. Abraham let some of the herdsmen have a supply of animals and return to Haran. Most of those who left Shechem with him either returned or found other means of caring for their families. Soon Abraham told the few who remained that they would move southward. As they traveled, food was in short supply and each day was as joyless as the previous one had been. Sarah thought to herself that Yahweh could give the land to someone else for she wanted none of it. At the same time she wondered whether she was wrong to have doubts. It even crossed her mind that Abraham and his father before him might not have received messages from Yahweh after all. For the first time she realized that she had lost her faith in the goddess she believed in as a child and felt her soul was empty. She expressed some of her conflicted thinking to her husband, who helped little in settling her mind. He held to his belief of a covenant with Yahweh, yet was torn as to whether they should remain in the land during this trying time or should move completely out of the country into Egypt, where he had heard the corn was tall and green. Perhaps he never made a decision; they just kept up the journey, slow though it was, until they found themselves crossing the Red Sea into Egypt.

How different the country was! Merchants besieged them with wares, which they were told were necessities of life. Food vendors called out to them and the country seemed full of high-energy, hard-driven people. Men eyed Sarah right off, making Abraham wonder if Yahweh was displeased that they left their own land. Coins were given for purchase of some of their animals and for one of the coins a man led them to a place where they could pitch their tents. Another coin brought food and water for the remaining beasts.

"Did you see how the men looked at you? One of them told me that the king gives a handsome reward to any person who brings a beautiful woman for his harem. If the woman has a husband, the king has him slaughtered so that by law the woman can be his since she has no man. Remember your promise to say that you are my sister should such harm befall us. It would not be an untruth after all."

"And Lot is your firstborn son?" Sarah mused, as though the whole idea was in the realm of impossibility.

The more they saw of Egypt the more enraptured they

were. It was a culture they had not seen even in their dreams. Lot was pressed into primary responsibility for their possessions while Abraham and Sarah spent their days walking wide-eyed around the land. They saw what the inhabitants called the pyramids and Abraham gazed as far as his eyes could see at the wonders and shook his head saying, "*It is not possible.*" The sphinx was even more impossible. Abraham and Sarah could almost understand why Egyptians worshipped the Nile when they first saw the "Great River of Egypt." They spent days traversing its banks and marveled at the junction of the Blue Nile and the White Nile at Khartoom. Egypt held so many enchantments for them that time moved swiftly.

When Abraham discovered that many learned men had schools and a teacher could be found for every interest, he made specific inquiries and found an aged seer familiar with Yahweh God. Abraham immediately became his pupil, which ended Sarah's outings with him. At the end of the first lesson, Abraham rushed to tell Sarah and Lot of his new found knowledge. He was disappointed. He let them know that the teacher accepted all gods, but was highly pleased with the learned one's knowledge of Yahweh. The first lesson dealt with the creation and none of the account was doubted by Abraham. Sarah pondered the creation story the next day and at noonday tried to talk with Lot about it, to no avail. The creation was important, sure, but not as important as how much they would be paid for the sheep, was the way he looked at the whole thing.

Abraham's story the second day was even more without. He had been told of God's created man being lonely even though he had a perfect world and even though God came down personally for a visit each day. Finally God made a woman for him. Sarah exclaimed, "*Oh, this part is good. A man is not at peace without a woman. A woman can do for a man what even God can not."*

Abraham paused only briefly before explaining. *"The woman was God's gift to man. You are my possession because God gave you to me. Wait, that is not all. The woman was his downfall. Because of her, he lost everything."* Then he told Sarah the rest of the lesson the seer had taught, only to have her say, *"If the woman can get the man to do something that Yahweh himself said not to do, I ask you, Who owns who?"*

One day while Abraham was away learning, Sarah ventured hardly more than a stone's throw, hoping to find some new delicacy to prepare for the evening meal. The merchant was very kind and asked her name and from whence she came. Within hours two men wearing insignia, which she surmised made them in the employ of the king, arrived at the tent and unceremoniously placed Sarah into a chariot, driving away with her. She was too stunned to ask many questions but did learn that she would be seen briefly by King Sensusert to see if he desired that she enter his harem. If she pleased him, then she would go through thirty days of preparation and beautification.

At the king's residence she was taken into his presence, just as the abductors had said. *"She pleases me well,"* was the response of the king. Then he inquired whether she had a husband and one of the men informed him that she lived with two men in two tents.

Without waiting to be asked, Sarah half-lied, *"The man is my brother and the younger one our nephew. That explains the two tents—the men's and myself."*

"Perhaps I may see you soon. I like to learn of other nations but I shall not touch you until the thirty days have elapsed."

Sarah was escorted to a large hall furnished with ornate recliners and beds, with huge bathing vats. Two women were luxuriating in the tubs, while attendants fussed over them, adding sweet savors and oils to the bathing water. The two women eyed Sarah carefully while one of the attendants welcomed her. She was first measured to be fitted with new garments and then the two attendants tested and examined her skin and hair. Sarah said little, being too overcome with fright, disbelief and exhilaration. At sundown another attendant brought her a meal of vegetables and fruits, some of which she had never seen before. She wondered if she might be in the creation garden, but knew she had no business being there. Next she was placed into a reclining position on a beautiful marble slab with her head extending over a vat. She wondered what was about to happen and was amazed when one of the girls began to pour water over her hair. *"Good hair,"* the girl said as she began to add sweet smelling soaps and gently wash her hair. Sarah never dreamed women could live like this and told herself she would think of Abraham tomorrow.

The next morning a maid came to announce that there was a family member present to visit. Sarah's attendant gave word that the family member could wait until the bath and grooming were completed and then Sarah would go to the visiting room. Several hours later she emerged from the bath to have beautification creams and powders applied and to be dressed in a form-revealing gown of fine silk. She was escorted to the visiting room to see an uncomfortable, out-of-place Abraham waiting. She preened and said, *"I hope my brother is in good health today."* The attendant told Sarah that a visit of thirty minutes was allowed each day and she would return for her at the expiration of the allotted time.

"Sarah, what have you done?" he asked anxiously.

"You mean to be here or to look like this?" she teased.

"You look like a Baal prostitute," he said in frustration.

"There are many mirrors and I have seen how I look.

Unless you say that I look beautiful, then this visit shall not continue and anyway I am about to cry."

Abraham looked longingly at her and said, *"I dare not touch you but I want to hold you and, yes, you do look beautiful. A husband should let his wife look this way all the time. But we must speak of other things. How did you come to be here and how can we get you away from here so that we can return to the land we should never have left?"*

"I have been presented to the king and he will not touch me nor enter me until I have gone through the thirty day period of purification. Meanwhile I am safe here but how to be released I do not know. Will you continue with your teacher?"

"Sarah, how can I think of anything but how to get you out of here and back where you belong and how to get us back to the land we never should have left?" he asked incredulously.

"You could just tell the king that you are my husband," she said with casualness that she did not feel.

"Do you want me dead? There has to be another way. We will have to depend on our God to save us. I shall come each morning and I shall pray Yahweh to rescue you and other times I shall busy myself with building up the flocks and gathering enough stuff to return home as soon as we can. I am told there has been rain. Sarah, do you pray to our God?" he asked.

"When there is a need," she answered honestly.

"There is a need," he said with a degree of desperation.

Sarah wanted to ask him what he was having to eat but she knew if he told her she would feel guilty about her own royal fare. She asked a bit cautiously if he would like to hear what had happened since she was taken from their tent and gave him a full account. They agreed that he would return the following day and that somehow Sarah would be released to him. When the attendant came to end the visit, she handed Abraham three changes of new raiment, as a gift from the king. Abraham tried to refuse and tried to question why, but the only response was *"the king ordered."*

Abraham came to see Sarah daily and almost each day he received a gift from the king—animals, silver, gold, raiment. Meantime, the fortunes of the king suffered reverses. The third day that Sarah was there the palace staff was thrown into hysteria with the discovery of fire in the second kitchen. Two days afterwards all the king's little ones became almost unto death with a childhood disease that usually passed with nothing more than a few days of lethargy. Next, a flash flood caused the drowning of ten prized sheep.

The king sent for Sarah one day and greeted her with a smile of approval and a *"Tell me, my dear, did you bring all these daily woes upon me?"* He saw her bewilderment and hastened to say, *"Of course not. One so lovely could only bring prosperity."* He asked about the nations where they had sojourned and Sarah told briefly of their move because of the drought. She sought safety in the talk by praising the wonders of Egypt, asking flattering questions about himself and his nation, and discussing the new foods she had been served. He asked the reaction of her brother to the gifts he had received and Sarah feared her voice may betray her when she responded, *"My brother is humbly grateful."* The king dismissed her with a *"We shall talk again soon."*

Each day for three weeks Abraham came and each day felt himself more distanced with his wife. Her hands became white and delicate as though they had never been made for scrubbing clothes in a stream, hulling hazelnuts or gathering beans. She truly looked the part of a queen and seemed to gracefully glide, erect and tall, towards him. He longed to reach out to her but told himself that queens did not touch ordinary herdsmen. He wondered if she did not prefer her new life and suggested that after the king knew her as a woman she would likely never return to him. His statement angered Sarah much and she glared at him, *"I am a wife, A Wife, I said, nothing more. That is all I will ever be. Now get me out of here."*

The king sent for Sarah again and told her right away that his wise men were suggesting that she had something to do with the tragedies his family was experiencing one after the other. He asked whether the wisemen were correct. Sarah prayed silently and responded cautiously, *"We believe in Yahweh, the one God. It is He that sends blessings and when we displease Him, He allows ills to befall us. You must ask yourself if you have displeased God."*

"If I have displeased any god, I beg forgiveness and ask that this curse be lifted," the king replied. *"The attendants tell me that your brother has visited you every day and that his gaze is not that of a brother as he looks long into your eyes. Is there anything that you should tell me?"*

"If there is anything that you should be told, then my brother is the one to tell you," she replied.

"Very well, then," said the king, *"tell your brother that I shall see him at the third hour on the morrow in the inner courtyard. The gatekeepers will expect him."*

Sarah was agitated the remainder of the day and sleep left her all night. She called much on Yahweh, though her fears remained. Soon after the third hour the following morning, a servant came to inform that Sarah was to be brought before the king and she was to be wearing her own clothing. Sarah took this to mean she would be leaving, but did not know whether it would be dead or alive.

She found that Abraham had already had an audience with the king and that the king, instead of being angry, was frightened. He had made Abraham gifts of silver, gold and more raiment. To Sarah the king said, *"Go with your husband, leave Egypt, and pray your God to lift the curse put upon me because of you.*" As Abraham took her arm to head towards freedom, the king, seeming to note that he had given Sarah no gift, reached among the female servant group to grab a girl of about seven years and place her hand in Sarah's, saying, *"train up this servant as your own maid."* The child looked longingly at her mother and tears came to the eyes of each of them but there was no protest.

Sarah led the child to their tent then instructed, *"Tonight you sleep at the end of my mat. When we return to our own land, you will have your own tent. On the morrow we pack our belongings and leave Egypt forever. There are many things you will be able to do and I shall instruct you in your tasks. We all have tasks, you know."*

Despite their time of separation, Abraham and Sarah talked long of Yahweh's doings and what it meant. They pondered the fact that their sojourn in Egypt had left them rich, even though they may have displeased their God. They agreed that it had been a time never to be forgotten and marveled at the glory of the nation. Abraham told Sarah that he had even been given information as to events in Ur, though certainly no specifics of their relatives. The city had swelled until the city walls had been moved outward on three sides. A learning center had been built at Obeid and a possibility existed that all male children might one day learn to read and write. *"There is prosperity all about but there is no worship for the true God,"* Abraham lamented.

"If I have need to hear of my mother, how deep must be the need of the child Hagar. I shall remember that in dealing with her," Sarah promised. The child was sleeping before Abraham and his "wife" retired to their mat to continue the celebration of her homecoming.

The long journey home seemed but short for the joy of the return. Once they passed through the Negeb, they could tell rain had come in adequacy and there was grass for the animals to graze for a time each morning. Finally, they came to the spot between Bethel and Ai where they dwelt earlier. There was much that required doing but Abraham sought out the altar built by him in days past and when he found it he worshipped the Almighty.

They remained at the Bethel-Ai location and Abraham and Lot set about to re-establish acquaintance with those who dwelt there. Lot apparently succeeded, for very shortly he advised that he had found a woman who pleased him and would be taking her to wife. He declined Sarah's offer of a wedding supper and the only way they knew the marriage had taken place was by the fact that Lot did not come home one night. The next day he brought his wife to the tent, tarrying hardly long enough for Sarah to greet her. Lot removed his tent, leaving Sarah feeling as if death had passed by.

The herds increased over the years and both Abraham and Lot had numerous men in their employ. As time went on Sarah tired of the herdsmen coming to the tent to complain that Lot's servants had driven them from the best pastures. Abraham was a peacemaker, but his "brotherly love" admonitions fell on unhearing ears.

Abraham told Sarah one evening that there was too much conflict between his herdsmen and Lot's men. He felt some of Lot's employees were of a base sort and it was becoming too difficult for his men not to retaliate. *"Wealth is not worth angry words,"* he said.

When Abraham returned the following evening, Sarah greeted him with, *"Your countenance tells me the day has been eventful but I am not able to tell whether I see happiness or sorrow."*

"Both," her husband replied. *"Some of both. I told Lot that there had to be an end to the strife between his herdsmen*

and mine, and that the best answer would be for our flocks to be separated. I told him that he could have his choice of whatever areas he wished and I would take what was left. He considered for a time and took the Jordan Valley."

"But that is the best land, is it not? Did you let him take the best, when it was you who cared for him all his life?"

"The choice of land is not important; Yahweh will take care of it. I grieve because I feel in my heart that we have lost Lot. I will not see him in the fields anymore, will not sit under a terebinth tree and rub its leaves on our tired limbs, will not watch the pleasure the growth of his flocks brings him. I feel as though I have lost my only son."

"I have an affection for Lot, too, but must you use the term, 'son?' Lot's wife is already giving him children but it seems Yahweh has cursed me with barrenness. What have I done that He has not smiled upon me?"

"Sarah, the years of our lives are not finished. Yahweh has a plan. He told me our heirs would be many and I live in that hope."

CHAPTER FIVE

The maid-child Hagar learned quickly and was a servant/companion to her mistress. Much of her time was spent attending Sarah's personal needs—fetching, brushing her hair, and buckling her sandals. Sarah was surprised when Abraham decided he too needed a personal servant. He set out in search of just the right man and settled on one Eliezer, a Syrian from Damascus, whom he took for a lifetime. Like Sarah's maid, Eliezer was respected and was a confidant but he was always aware that his station in life was beneath that of the master.

Abraham was blessed of Yahweh and grew richer each year, yet claimed no title or position for himself. He was surrounded by many city-states, each headed by a king, several smaller than that of Abraham's mastery. He made it a point to meet and talk with all the kings near and far, primarily to tell of his belief in the one God and as a peacemaker. He talked to Sarah of his distress over the wickedness of some of these fiefdoms and of the fact that Lot had chosen the worst. He was heartened, however, to find some who believed in the true God, particularly in Salem, where King Melchizedek was also a priest.

King Chedorlaomer of Edom was the strongest of the kings and he required a tribute each year of the other nations. Finally after twelve years, the kings of Sodom, Gomorrah, Admah, Zeboiim and Bela had had enough and rebelled. They attacked King Chedorlaomer's army in the Salt Sea Valley, which valley was full of asphalt pits. Chedorlaomer's men put them to rout and as they fled many fell into the pits and the others hid themselves in the mountains. As victorious armies want to do, they plundered the conquered cities of Sodom and Gomorrah and took Lot captive from the city of Sodom. One servant was able to flee to Abraham to give him the news and beg for help. Abraham called together his servants who were of the age and condition to fight, a number totaling three hundred eighteen. He organized them military style and they set out in pursuit of the captives. He halted his army at Dan, realizing they were close on the conquers and when darkness fell they attacked and chased the captors as far as Hobah, before they released all that had been taken. It was a joyous and grateful Lot who fell on his uncle's neck and said, *"We are all here—my family, my servants and my belongings."*

Daylight brought a strange sight of men, women and children, all loaded down with possessions, trying to drive laden cattle, singing and shouting of their freedom.

As they returned, King Melchizedek brought bread and wine for Abraham, and Abraham with the authority of a king himself, proclaimed that one-tenth of all that had been retrieved should be given to the priest as a thank offering to the one true God. Then the King of Sodom asked Abraham to keep all the goods and return only the people to him, but Abraham declined lest it be said that he had made Abraham rich.

Sarah and the women were much relieved to see their men returning home and to find that not one had been lost. Sarah did not know how the other women greeted their men, but she gave hers a warm kiss and a *"I did not marry a warrior. Will you please remember forever that I married a herdsman."*

Abraham was humbled by his military victory and prayed to God that the wicked people who had been freed from their captors would realize that it was God who had saved them. He hoped Lot would impress on them the source of their rescue and perhaps he did for there was peace thereafter.

Abraham was known for his wealth, his wisdom and his worship of Yahweh. Sarah was known for her beauty and pitied for her barrenness. Whenever she wept in Abraham's arms, he always reminded her that Jehovah God, Yahweh himself, had told him over and over that his heirs would be many and would possess the land.

It was the custom when a covenant was entered into between two kings or other parties that an animal be killed and divided according to the terms of the agreement. If the parties were to share equally in the covenant, then the animal was divided into half. The parts were laid on the ground near each other and the participants would walk between and around them to seal the covenant. Often they removed their sandals to add to the sacredness of the agreement.

Sarah was not present when God entered into a covenant with Abraham and she had difficulty accepting it the way Abraham related it to her. According to him, he followed God's instructions to kill and divide in half a heifer, a female goat and a ram. He also killed a dove and a young pigeon and arranged them on the ground with the animal parts. Instead of walking among them, a deep sleep fell on Abraham and in his sleep he saw a smoking firepot and a flaming torch move among and around the animals. The pot signified that his descendants would have a dark period in their history but the flaming torch that followed foretold good years. God had again said that the covenant would be with Abraham and his heirs, who would be as numerous as the stars in the heavens. Sarah suggested the entire incident was a dream, but Abraham offered to take her the next day to see what the vultures had left of the carcasses.

The idea came to Sarah slowly and she turned it over in her mind, day after day. She rationalized, "If Hagar is mine and if she has a child by my husband, then the child will belong to me and my husband." The more she thought of it the more she became convinced that the idea was born of, or at least acceptable to, Yahweh.

Sarah waited for just the right moment to propose the idea to Abraham. He was shocked at first but could follow Sarah's reasonings. He reflected that God had promised him an heir but he could not recall offhand that the same was said of Sarah. He could not find it within himself to think of Hagar as a wife. To do that he would have to sleep with her the same number of nights he slept with Sarah. He and Sarah had always shared the same mat, but that would be over and she would have to have a separate tent to keep count of the nights spent with each wife. He would have to have a tent of his own for those nights when he desired neither. If he considered her a mere concubine she would be like Sarah's mother and the child would be reared knowing little of either Sarah or him. From what source did Yahweh intend his heirs to come? He finally reached a decision, right or wrong, that he would sleep with Hagar only until she was with child and that otherwise she would occupy her own tent next to that of his and Sarah's; but she could call herself a wife.

As yet no one had approached Hagar with the proposal

and Sarah did so delicately. *"Hagar,"* she said, *"The King of Egypt gave you to me, remember?"* Hagar nodded and Sarah went on. *"You are my possession but I think of you as more than my maid."* Sarah realized that she was getting near the edge of truthfulness but she continued. *"I think of you almost as my daughter. You have observed that the Lord has shut up my womb and I have not been able to give your master a son. Listen carefully; if you are mine and my husband goes in to you, then you will be giving both him and me a child. This will not be forced upon you. God has promised us heirs and I believe that in this way both you and I will be a part of God's plan. Think about it and let me know what you decide."*

Hagar had questions a few days later as to her relationship to Abraham, and Sarah answered for all, *"You will not be considered a harlot nor a concubine. You will be considered a wife until you conceive. After that the marriage will be over and if you wish, he will give you a bill of divorcement."*

Hagar pondered her plight and reasoned that should she say no, her mistress was well within her rights to force her. Too, she had come to believe that knowing a man was pleasurable and this would be her only opportunity to find out for herself. Lastly, the reason to proceed with the plan was to fulfill the purpose of creation, to bear a child. That way she would be of more value than her mistress and would certainly be elevated in the eyes of her master and in her own eyes.

Abraham slept with Hagar on five consecutive nights during the period of her fertility, and she was glad when it was finally all over. Abraham told her he did nothing to increase the pleasure for her, lest she later go awhoring. Sarah was more anxious than Hagar as she awaited the outcome and was much overjoyed when she learned that they were to become a mother. In fact, she began to treat Hagar with deference and assigned some of Hagar's usual tasks to other servants. Hagar had never felt that she was of any worth whatsoever, and suddenly she became very important in her own eyes. Heretofore obedient, she took to lolling on pillows during the day, not moving when Sarah pointed out an undone task. Resentment between the two women reached the breaking point when Hagar responded to Sarah's command with, *"You do it. I must take care of myself for I am having my husband's child, you know."* Sarah's anger boiled as she rushed outside screaming for Abraham. He ran towards her thinking someone had surely died to hear her lash out, *"God is going to punish you for what you have done to me. That servant girl despises me now that she is going to have your child and the whole mess is your fault!"*

He threw up his hands in exasperation, saying, *"Wait a minute! You can not blame me. This was your idea. You handle this with your maid. It's up to you."*

Sarah picked up a shepherd's staff as she returned to the tent and began to strike Hagar on the shoulders and backside. Both women were screaming loudly as Sarah chased Hagar beyond the oak of Mambe near where their tents were pitched. Both women saw Abraham observing in the distance and each thought he should come to her aid, but he only looked at them with disdain. Sarah finally turned back, while Hagar continued to run.

Hagar kept going until she fell from exhaustion, her body shaking. She was hot and her throat was dry but for the most part she was frightened of what should become of her. As she raised herself from the ground, she thought it must be a miracle for there within steps of where she fell was a clear, cool water spring. She drank her fill and washed her face, raising her skirt to dry herself. She suddenly lowered her skirt and seated herself ladylike on a rock for she beheld a gentleman by her side. He addressed her, *"Hagar, Sarah's maid, where are you going and where have you been?"* She almost fell into a faint for she realized the voice was that of an angel and if he knew her name and station in life he must be from Yahweh and if so, then Yahweh was real. He was indeed the one true God and would not only understand her predicament, but would care for her and she need not die alone in the wilderness.

Trembling in awe, she answered, *"I am running away from my mistress."* Then, as though to justify her action and just in case the angel did not know everything, she repeated, *"I am running away from my mistress because she beats me."*

The angel, in the calmest yet more authoritative voice said, *"Go back to your mistress and stay there. The child developing within you is indeed a male child and you shall call his name Ishmael, which means 'God hears.' The child will become a mighty hunter, skilled with the bow and arrow. He will be an outdoorsman and of him will I make a great nation. Now return to your mistress."*

In the fullness of her time, Hagar delivered a male child and he was called Ishmael. Sarah was at Hagar's side as the midwives attended her. It was Sarah who laid the newborn into Abraham's arms and said, *"God has given us a son."* When she saw the child suckling at Hagar's breast, she realized who the mother really was and went aside and wept.

Ishmael was a sturdy, handsome child who learned early that Abraham was his father. He toddled behind him as he walked. Hagar called Sarah "your other mother" when talking to her son, but Ishmael was loyal to the one who suckled him. Seeing him with Hagar only heightened Sarah's desire to birth a child herself. Observing Hagar nurse her child made Sarah's own breast feel full with an empty ache.

Some time later Abraham rushed inside to tell Sarah that Jehovah God had appeared to him that day and had reaffirmed the covenant agreement. God had told him once more that his heirs would be many and that among them would be kings and men of great importance and that the land of Canaan would belong to his descendants.

Sarah said, *"Tell me once more what your part of the covenant requires."*

Abraham went silent for a time and then answered, *"We are to . . . . to follow after God and keep all his commands."* Here he stopped before going on. *"And . . . as a sign of our faithfulness . . . . every male in our family now and in all future generations is to be circumcised. This will signify that they are a part of the covenant, too."*

"Circumcised? What does that mean?" she asked somewhat casually.

"It means a purification . . . a purification of the heart, soul and body. In it . . . uh . . . the foreskin of the male's member is cut off and Jehovah God says this should happen when the child is eight days old."

Sarah frowned a question mark, indicating doubt of everything she had heard, before she said, *"Is it not easier to worship the sun god? If I were a man, I would find it much more desirable. Surely, Abraham, you have mistaken the message of your God."*

He assured, *"There is no mistake. God came to me in the form of an angel and I heard His words plainly. Those who fail to bear the mark will have no part of the covenant. Sarah, I have fear and joy within me. The angel said more. He said he would bless me and then he called your name and said that he would make you the mother of nations. I asked that Ishmael be blessed and walk in God's ways and ". . . .* suddenly Abraham buried his face in her breasts and began weeping. She held him, full of wonder and concern over the holy revelation until he finally could half utter the words, *"God said we would have a son. You will conceive and bear a son!"*

Sarah comforted him as a mother would a child and finally held his face in her hands as she said sadly, *"Oh my husband, I am full of regret and sorrow and I long to comfort you but I fear you have an illness of the mind. Or perhaps you worship a God who has gone mad. Look at me! I am not your fourteen-year-old bride. Do you not see an old woman? You know that it has ceased to be with me after the manner of women and not even God could give me a child now?"*

Abraham remonstrated, *"Sarah, you are more beautiful than ever. I see no lines on your face. I have told you that Yahweh is a God of miracles. With Him, nothing is impossible."*

Sarah asked within herself, "Then why has He not heard my prayers?" Aloud she said, *"I am truly grateful that you have a son. The promise of many descendants can be believed. I only regret that I failed you because God shut up my womb."*

"We shall see," Abraham said with a twinkle in his eye. Then he set about his son, his servants and all his male employees to explain to them the covenant relationship with God.

The women did not understand it as the men went off alone and later struggled back, wounded and bleeding, the younger ones screaming in pain as they carefully cupped their members. At first the women had difficulty in keeping their laughter inside and as the men returned the women kept their hands over their mouths to hide their smiles of ridicule and joy in this particular suffering. Later the women found sheep tending, milking, feeding and humoring helpless males more than they bargained for. Abraham found it prideful and an indication of serious commitment to the covenant.

Abraham ordered two of the women servants to fetch the bucket that contained the severed foreskins and bury them under the oak.

CHAPTER SIX

Sarah wished Abraham would forget about a baby for her, but he did not. She turned his talk aside when she could, or brought up Ishmael's name when he spoke of descendants. *"Your son is to be called Isaac,"* he instructed her one-day. *"Jehovah God has given him that name already. Your son will be great but so will Ishmael. God has revealed to me that Ishmael will be the father of twelve mighty men, but it will be your son who will enter into the covenant with God."*

"When you are fully recovered from the circumcision will you be more of a man? Do you think you can give me a child then?" Sarah teased.

"It will not be because of the circumcision, but because God said it would happen."

Soon thereafter on a hot day when the sun was directly overhead, Abraham sat in the shade of the tent seeking to cool himself. His eyes were drawn to a noise in the distance and he looked to see three strangers walking in his direction. Having earlier experienced messengers from God, he wondered whether these also might be angels or whether they were spies passing themselves off as men of importance. He wanted to take no chance and immediately went towards them, urging them to pause to cool themselves. At once he brought water for the washing of dust from their feet. Then he went inside the tent and told Sarah to hasten in preparing bread for the travelers. Next he rushed to take the fatted calf, always in reserve for just such occasions, and instructed a servant to slaughter it and prepare enough for the three visitors.

As they waited for the meat to roast, Abraham brought cool water, then cheese and milk. When the bread and meat were ready, Abraham graciously served his guests and they ate without revealing where they were going or from whence they came. Abraham's curiosity was high and he was not able to decide whether they were of God or mere men. Finally one asked, *"Where is Sarah, thy wife?"* Abraham reckoned in his mind that strangers would not know the name of his wife and was sure he was in the presence of holy beings.

"In the tent," he replied.

Now Sarah was just inside the tent, hiding herself, but listening so as not to miss what was said.

"Next year," the spokesman of the three continued, *"You and Sarah will have a son."*

Sarah laughed within herself at such a preposterous idea and told herself that she could understand where Abraham was getting his strange talk.

Just then Abraham called her outside at the behest of the man. Women did not go outside in the presence of strangers and Sarah hesitated before she slowly came from the tent. Observing the rule not to address a woman who had a husband, the man asked of Abraham, *"Why did she laugh?"*

Sarah was startled and began denying that she had laughed. The man, still looking at Abraham, said, *"Is anything too hard for God? Next year about this time, Sarah will give birth to a son. And she did laugh!"*

Sarah stood speechless as the men graciously thanked Abraham for his hospitality and started down the road towards Sodom, with Abraham walking a ways with them.

"Who were they?" Sarah asked when he finally returned. *"Why were there three of them? One did all the talking. You know God would not have sent three, would he?"*

"Sarah, two were angels and one was God himself. Now you must surely believe what I have been telling you!"

"We will know ere long. If they speak true, I will be with child in three months. Until then I make no decision. Should they be foretelling a truth, I will know that our God is mightier than any force on earth. I will bow down before Him and raise up to praise His name all the days of my life. If nothing happens, which is what I believe, those men were spies and will come again to do us ill. What did you talk about after you left? You must have gone half way to Sodom."

Abraham said grimly, *"These are touchy times. God told me that he was going to Sodom and Gomorrah and if things are as bad as has been told to Him, He is going to destroy the cities and all the people therein. I did not mention Lot by name but I had to do everything in my means to save our near-kinsman. So I tried with God the trick you use on me when you think I do not notice. God forgive me, but since you get what you want, I tried it. I told God that I had always thought Him to be a fair God, but if he killed everybody in Sodom that would not be fair to the good people, to be killed along with the bad. Then I asked, 'If you find fifty good people, would you spare the city for their sake?' Now all the time I doubted, based on what I had heard, that there were fifty righteous people there, but God agreed that He would spare Sodom if he could find fifty righteous people."*

"*What happened then?*" Sarah wanted to know.

"*Well, I then said, 'What if you do not find quite fifty good folk, say you find only forty-five, will you spare the city for their sake?' and God agreed. I felt I was doing well with influencing God, but He might have been beating me at my own game of play. He may have known from the outset how many righteous ones were there. I felt very powerful to be trying to talk God out of something, so I said, 'Well, suppose you find as few as thirty good people?' Can you believe God agreed to that? You can be sure I was very cautious but I said, "What will you do if you find as few as twenty righteous people?"*

"*Abraham, surely you did not say any such!*" Sarah said in disbelief.

"*Not only that,*" he responded, "*I apologized and asked if He would let me ask one last thing—and then I asked if He would destroy the town if ten righteous people lived there. And God said that if he found as many as ten he would not destroy the town. That was as far as I thought I had better go but surely Lot has brought that many people to the worship of our God. There must be ten good people in Sodom!*"

"*If there are not as many as ten good people, the city should be destroyed,*" was Sarah's comment.

But Abraham was concerned for Lot. He dared not try to outrun God and find Lot to warn him to flee. He could hardly eat his meal at sundown and paced outside the tent with his face towards Sodom, not knowing what, if anything, he should expect to see. The moon was high when he went into the tent and lay down to sleep fitfully until daybreak. He was out before the sun was up and all was as it had been the previous dawn. Suddenly he began to call to Sarah and she rushed out, along with the servants, to see an unbelievable sight, which he knew was an act of a fair God.

Great walls of smoky fire first came down, with flames reaching towards the earth. Within minutes the fire reversed and leapt from the ground upward. Even as far away as Sodom and Gomorrah were, faint wails and screams, mixed with the agonizing sounds of animals burning alive, added to the visual horror. They stood like stone pillars in their places, mute and bewildered. Then Abraham spoke, *"I must go to learn whether our kinsman was spared. He may need help of me."*

"Abraham, do not go," Sarah begged, clutching his raiment.

"I must go," he replied, as he went inside and got his outer robe and staff and set off in the direction of the conflagration.

Hagar and Ishmael were nearby and Ishmael asked question after question about the event they had witnessed. His mother looked at Sarah, inviting her to complete the explanation. Sarah did not usually engage in much conversation with the boy but she did tell him that God was destroying the cities because of their great evil.

Now a consuming fear had come upon all Abraham's household and the fear was directed towards God and focused on their own state of righteousness, or unrighteousness. There was much concern expressed for Lot and whether he had been spared. Many of the family, including Ishmael, hurried out to meet Abraham when they saw him approaching at early afternoon. They wanted to hear first of Lot and his family and then what the rubble of the cities looked like. Abraham immediately told them that Lot had been spared. He and his two youngest daughters were alive but his married daughters and their husbands had perished. Lot's wife escaped the fire, but had been turned to a pillar of rock salt outside the city because of her disobedience.

Ishmael interrupted with, *"Isn't that better than the fire? I am never going to disobey Yahweh."*

Abraham put his arm about the boy's shoulder and said to him, *"Son, that is my daily prayer."* Then he told how he had been met by an angel who had made him aware that Lot and his two daughters had been led by God to the village of Zoar, adding, *"I am glad that I did not have to go to Sodom for the stench sickened me from miles away. I went to Zoar and talked to Lot and early on the morrow we will take provender for him."*

When he and Sarah were alone, he said, *"We knew the Sodomites were evil, but from what Lot told me we did not know the half. The men had no respect for women, nor for each other. The marriage bed was defiled without shame. The name of God struck no awe in the hearts of the people and it seems their only thoughts were of eating and drinking in riotous living. After the angels left here, they journeyed on towards Sodom and, as it was, Lot sat at the city gate. He was always gracious to strangers, you know, and he begged the men to lodge with him. They declined, saying they did not wish to be a bother and would just sleep in the streets. Of course, Lot knew what would happen if they did so, and he insisted even more. They agreed to go home with him and Lot made them most honored guests. That evening Lot served them a banquet and all was well until there was a rap at the door. Lot looked out and there were an untold number of men, some hardly more than boys, about his house. They demanded that he send the visitors out because they wanted to know them. Lot, of course, refused. He went outside and closed the door behind him and tried to reason with them but a mob of madmen is hard to counter. They began to try to get to the door and finally Lot offered them his two virgin daughters instead. The men began to scream against Lot, saying that he was a newcomer who was trying to tell them what was right and take away their pleasures. Then they became violent and began to shove Lot. In fact, he might not have saved his life had not the angels opened the door and hastily pulled him inside. The mob began to try to break the door, but they were struck by sudden blindness and were groping about in startled confusion. When they finally left, the two angels told Lot that Sodom and Gomorrah were so evil they stank in the nostrils of God and were to be destroyed. They told Lot to tell his family to flee the oncoming destruction immediately. He went to tell his sons-in-law to take their families and run but they paid no mind, sure he did not speak truth."*

Sarah shook her head and said, *"It has always been so and always will be, I suppose, that people perish because they do not heed a warning."*

"I have much grief for Lot and yet he is aware that he should never have moved toward Sodom. I suppose his wife wanted a house instead of a tent and now half his family is gone! I offered him to return to our tent but he only thanked me. I do believe he cannot be as prideful of his daughters as I am of my son when it comes to righteousness."

CHAPTER SEVEN

Abraham was still on edge about Lot and he almost welcomed the suggestion of the herdsmen that the pastureland had been grazed out and it would be profitable to move southward so the grass could re-establish itself. All of them were accustomed to taking down, packing up, setting up and unpacking, so it was just a break in the routine of daily monotony, to travel nearly forty miles south and settle between Kadesh and Shur.

Abraham, as was his custom, went to explore the town of Gerah and was having a pleasant day meeting the townspeople, when mention was made of the beautiful lady in his family. He should have thought twice but he casually said, *"Yes, I am often told that my sister is beautiful."* Now Sarah had retained her beauty, age adding a dimension of poise and grace that made her more alluring. King Abimilech of Gerah, himself of middle age, was delighted to learn that she was not the man's wife and sent for her that very day.

That night the king had a dream, in which God said, *"King Abimilech, you are dead meat; for that woman you thought such a beauty is the man's wife."*

"But he said she was his sister and she said likewise. I did not mean to do anything wrong," the king assured in his dream.

God's reply was, *"It was I who kept you from sleeping with her already. Restore her to her husband for he is a prophet and if you do sin with the prophet's wife, you and your household will suffer death. Moreover, I have closed the wombs of all your household and your flocks and none shall bear until this woman is restored to her husband."*

Early the next morning the king called all his servants and told them of his dream. He sent for Abraham and inquired whether his dream was from God. Abraham answered, *"I knew not that you had respect to God and thought this was a godless place. All my life I have had difficulty with men desiring my wife and always have been afraid men who did not know God would kill me for her. We made a pact soon after I took her to wife that she would say she was my sister; a half-truth for we had the same father."*

The king replied, *"You have wronged me! I was almost killed because I believed your word. You would let me be punished of God because of sin of which I was innocent?"* Then the king took sheep and oxen and servants and gold and gave them to Abraham. He offered him use of any in his kingdom and asked Abraham to bless his household. Then he had his servants restore Sarah to her husband, but he also had a few words of reprimand for her as he sent them on their way.

Sarah was not as overjoyed at the restoration as the first time and as soon as they were alone she looked at him sternly and said, *"How many times do you think this will work for you? I would have stayed except it is getting near the time the angel said you would cause me to be with child. The king might have been just as able!"*

Sarah determined that if she did not conceive it would not be for lack of opportunity. Abraham did not disagree. She wondered how she would know if she had conceived, which did present something of a problem. She told Hagar that there was a possibility and asked for first signs from her. Then she began to abandon her usual responsibilities, being consumed with an "am I" or "am I not." The servants did a bit of laughing at such a preposterous notion that Sarah could be with child after so many years but subtle hints soon convinced Sarah that she believed in angels. Her breasts began to swell and become tender, she did not desire food on arising in the mornings and she just felt different inside. At the first protrusion of her normally flat belly, she became ecstatic. She insisted that she and Abraham go alone to build an altar and worship the God with whom nothing is impossible.

The day that quickening occurred Sarah decided that a celebration should take place requiring two fatted calves, one for the household feast and one to sacrifice in worship.

Sarah took note that Hagar seemed not to change in her attitude towards her mistress, which was surprising seeing that her son would no longer be the sole heir of his father. Sarah told herself that she should not act differently towards Hagar nor Ishmael, though their places in the family would be lowered with the birth of her son.

All was readied for parturition and midwives were brought in ahead of time. On the set laying-in date a healthy male child was delivered of Sarah. The midwives submerged him in warm water for cleansing, carefully rubbed him with salt and wrapped him in swaddling clothes. When the child was eight days old, his father took him aside and performed the act of circumcision while the mother stayed in her own tent and wept for the pain her baby would feel and at the joy she felt in giving her husband a son. Soon father returned the screaming infant, placed him in Sarah's arms and declared, *"His name is Isaac."*

Sarah responded, *"Yes, let his name be Isaac, which means laughter. Truly I did laugh within myself when the angel said 'I will give you a son in your old age.' May this child fill our days with laughter and may we praise our God for this birth and dedicate this child to walk in God's ways."*

Sarah mothered too much but she cared not for she had waited too long for the opportunity. The child's hair and skin were lighter than his older half-brother. He was just as handsome but they bore no resemblance. No nursemaid was necessary since Sarah herself attended every need. Small wonder that the child Isaac was always at his mother's side and was obedient in everything asked of him. He learned quickly and could recite prayers before most his age could talk. He was suckled at his mother's breast until he was three years old, a good six months longer than most children. As was the custom, a great celebration was held on the day the child was weaned. All the household who could leave their work at mid-afternoon, along with a few townspeople, assembled themselves to praise the child on entering the next stage of growth and to enjoy the festivities and food. Sarah had gone into the city with Abraham's servant, Eliezer, to the shop of one skilled in spinning and sewing and had a special robe made for her son's celebration. Many times during the event Isaac was told how handsome and how mature he looked in this new robe. Isaac was a bit timorous as a rule but he was obviously proud of his new raiment for after all no one else had anything so fine. He strutted and pranced near the guests to the proud laughter of his mother.

Sarah just happened to glance towards Hagar's tent and saw Ishmael strutting from behind a tree, mocking little

Isaac in his new robe. Rage swept across her and she had to collect herself before she could face the guests and be halfway polite as she ended the observance. No sooner was everyone out of sight than she marched to Abraham and demanded, *"You get rid of that slave girl and her son now! I will not have him inheriting from you with my son Isaac. I mean now!"* she screamed as she turned from him.

Abraham was taken aback and stunned into silence, but thoughts piled up. The idea was impossible! Didn't she realize that Ishmael was his son, too? It would be sin to turn out any child to perish, to say nothing of one's own son. He would not do it! Nothing could make him do such a deed. He would pray God for the strength to calm his wife and settle the matter.

That night he avoided Sarah, as she avoided him. He poured out his anguish to Jehovah God. The response he got stunned him as much as Sarah's outburst but it came in a resigned, reassuring way. God said, *"Yes, turn Hagar and her son out. That is the only way you will have any peace. Do not worry. I will take care of the boy for your sake. Isaac is the son through whom my promise will be fulfilled but I will bless Ishmael and make of him a great nation also."*

The next morning Abraham rose with a heavy heart and instructed that a double portion of the day's bread be baked. Then he went to Hagar and wept as he told her she and Ishmael were to be cast out that day. He related God's promise to her but it was hard for her to think of anyone's care when the person she most depended on in life had just withdrawn that care. The only thing she asked was, "Why?" Hagar sat on her mat in defeat and anger as she gave her son the news. She knew she was too blunt in telling him but was encouraged by his calm, *"I know my father loves me. It is mistress Sarah, isn't it?"*

Abraham could not face Ishmael and waited until he saw him leave the tent before going to Hagar with a supply

of bread and a large pitcher of water and wishing her
Jehovah's protection. The news had spread fast and the
household staff, especially Eliazer, stole a minute to express
their sorrow and wish them safety. Hagar called her son and
they set out with no destination in mind.

Hagar was still in a state of disbelief and could only
mutter, *"Why? Why? Why?"* She did not call on Yahweh
God for He should have kept this from happening if He
cared for mortal beings. After all, she had gone back and
been a faithful servant, had she not? She had not crossed
'that woman' and she also gave Abraham a son and could
see no way she deserved this. She did not understand how
Abraham let 'that woman' tell him what to do.

Hagar and Ishmael wandered aimlessly until sundown
and Ishmael found a clump of bushes that would provide a
good place to sleep the night. They had bread and a small
drink of water, for the jar was already half empty. *"Would
that I had never left Egypt,"* Hagar cried to the stars. Ishmael
knew his mother came from Egypt, but that was all he
knew. He asked her to tell him about how she came to
leave her home and Hagar relived her life as they lay near
each other on the warm sand.

The next day was much the same except for having less
bread and less water. By the third day the water was gone
and the bread that remained could hardly feed two birds.
By the fifth day they could walk no more than a few steps,
mostly for lack of water. Ishmael thought he was too old to
cry but Hagar knew she was not. She told him to stretch
out under the shade of a bush and she walked, stumbling a
distance and fell to the ground praying, "Spare me from
seeing him die!" She wondered how tears could come when
she was sure there was not an ounce of fluid left in her
body. She prayed that her strength would hold out long
enough for her to be able to bury her son. She could tolerate

the idea of birds pecking away at her carcass but not his. And she prayed to die before the birds began. Then from the distance she heard him cry and her pain was more than all the other grief of her life bound together.

The voice came from the air above; a voice she had heard in this same wilderness years ago. Was it real? Then she heard the voice call her name. *"Hagar, I have heard the cries of the lad. Do not despair for I will care for you. Go and embrace your son for I will make of him a great nation. Do not fear and do not doubt."*

And then God opened Hagar's eyes and lo and behold there was a spring of water only a few feet away. *"Oh, God of the water spring, thank you."* She shouted, as she called Ishmael, took a long drink and filled her pitcher with enough water to restore her son. They drank and splashed water on their parched bodies and then drank some more. *"Our lives have been restored to us,"* she said, *"yours because of greatness ahead, mine, why?"*

CHAPTER EIGHT

Abraham continued to become even more wealthy and he became well known throughout the territory. Times were beginning to change, as all the land was no longer available to him and his herds. A man could claim ownership to land but in truth he owned only that which he could protect from others. There continued to be ample grazing space, even though some of the land might be claimed by a king or self-made landowner. When people spoke of Abraham, they talked of how his God was with him and prospered him and they spoke of the beauty of his wife. He gained respect, at the same time engendering fear because of the size of his household and of his wealth.

One day when they were making their home near Beer-Sheba, King Abimiliech and his army captain, Phicol, came to call on Abraham. They greeted him as though he were a mighty king and asked that Abraham continue to be on friendly terms with them. The king told him that advancing age made it obvious that his son would soon become king in his stead and asked Abraham to be friendly with him, too. Abraham could understand his efforts to protect his son and there was a long conversation by two doting fathers, expressing pride in their offspring.

Abraham was willing to enter such a covenant but said to the king, *"Does this mean that your servants will take no other wells from me by force?"*

The king was surprised, having no knowledge of such behavior by his men. They walked to the well in question, passing near Abraham's flock. Abraham selected sheep and oxen as a gift to the king. Then he took seven choice ewe lambs and put them by themselves away from the others. The king asked why he was doing this and Abraham said, *"These are in payment for the well, if I owe anything for it. Let it be known to all that the well belongs to me."*

"On oath I so swear," said the king.

The next day Abraham and Eliezer planted tamarisk trees beside the well and called it the Well of Beer-Sheba.

Sarah never regretted the absence of Hagar and Ishmael, and even Abraham found that she was rarely disagreeable since they were gone. Or should her pleasant nature be attributed to motherhood?

Abraham had loved Ishmael, but his love for Isaac was deeper than he believed a father's love for a son could be. He began each day with praise to his God for the gift of his son and asked for divine protection and that he himself be a suitable pattern for Isaac. Life was idyllic.

But who can expect all to be pleasant and without demands forever? Abraham told Sarah one day that he was going to take their son and go into the mountains to sacrifice to God. The intensity of his voice and on his face made Sarah say that she would like to go too. Abraham tried gently to discourage her but it took a firm, *"Jehovah himself told me to take Isaac and two servants and none else."* She understood the packing of foods and wood for the fire but she did not understand why they should go such a distance as Moriah, nor why Abraham was so morose. They set out early the next morning and returned near dusk six days later; six days that had seen Sarah agitated and confused.

A servant alerted Sarah that the returnees had been spotted in the distance and she rushed to meet them, as her son ran towards her outstretched arms. Isaac greeted her with, *"Father did not have to sacrifice me. Yahweh provided a lamb."* There was no embrace for Abraham from his wife. *"I wanted to tell you about it first,"* was his explanation.

It was only after the two adults were alone that Sarah said venomously, *"So you were going to act like the heathens! You were going to sacrifice my son to please your God! Sacrificing a child is evil! Jehovah does not expect, accept or demand any such behavior. Abraham, I do not understand you! I hate you!"*

Abraham replied as calmly as he could, *"Hate and killings are blood brothers. Both are wrong. God has appeared to me six times in the past telling me that my son would become a great nation and that through him the world would be blessed. Then God told me to take my son, my only son and sacrifice him as a burnt offering on a mountain in Moriah. No, I did not understand it and no I did not tell you. What would you have done?"*

Sarah answered, *"I do not know. But I know you would not have left with him."*

Abraham went on, *"But I had to follow Jehovah's command. I think it was not a test, for God knew what I would do, but a confirmation for me that as much as I love that boy, Jehovah comes first. And to see the trust he has in me! He trusts me like I trust Jehovah; No, I was more afraid than he was. When I laid him on that altar, he just looked at me with no fear whatsoever, for he had asked me where the lamb was and I told him that God would provide it. He has learned the lesson I learned years ago, but sometimes forget, that our God will keep His part of the covenant when we follow Him. I believe this was Jehovah's way of teaching our son that lesson. Sarah, the voice of God was beyond all wonder! I was ready to sacrifice my only son, my beloved, my innocent son but God stayed my hand when He called my name. I heard a bleat and I did not even have to look. There with his horns tangled in a thorn bush was a ram. What a mighty God we serve! Oh Sarah, I couldn't let you go but I wish you could have been there! It was another reminder of God with us. He has done so many good things for us. But I needed to experience Him again. I call on Him when times are troubled but I may be apt to forget Him in good times."*

CHAPTER NINE

Hagar and Ishmael stayed by the spring until the next day and Ishmael was able to trap a dove, which he baked in the embers of a fire started from pieces of shale rock he found in the sand. He also found mullusk and five scrawny berries. Hagar felt the hand of God leading in the direction away from the sun, so they filled their pitcher and their stomachs with water and set off.

Soon after mid-day they came to a discernable roadway and were soon overtaken by a traveler on a camel. He thought they might find shelter at Lachish, a village not many miles distant.

Hagar was sure Jehovah had intervened with the chief settler of the village for he was in need of a family servant and a youth who knew how to tend sheep. They worked for only their food and shelter but they received something more valuable than wages. They got first-hand news from Egypt and a hope of being able to go there some day. The man who sheltered them was Emuel, who was also a trader who went south to Egypt twice a year and as far north as

Sumuri. He had news of happenings in Egypt, including
that at the death of King Sunusert, his son become King
Sunusert II. Better still, there was a possibility that Hagar
and Ishmael could accompany a caravan to Egypt the
following year if they had a small amount of gold. Some
weeks later, Emuel entered an agreement that if they worked
for one year then he would give them gold and they could
accompany the caravan on the journey.

Hagar did her very best and no one in the family could
fault her for the quality, nor yet the quantity of her work.
Ishmael spent his time with the sheep and learned their ways
and the ways of the seasons. His mind was always hungry
and when he was not learning from the earth or the sky,
there were shepherds to share information and skills. That
is how he came to know the art of bow making and how he
became such a skilled archer that he could bring down a
bird in flight and once he felled a marauding wolf he saw
stalking a lamb. He asked permission to sleep outdoors with
the sheep and sometimes did not return to his mother for
weeks on end. He washed himself in the streams and fed
well on fruits of the wild, game from the kill and milk
from the she-goats.

As the year ended and the time came for the payment
of their wages, Ishmael decided to let his mother go alone
to Egypt since she would be safe. He would give her half
his gold for her use there and he would take the other half
to hire the teacher Emuel knew so that he could learn to
read and write the word pictures of the Egyptian language.
His father had seen to it that he was literate in their own
writings, but he felt that was only part of his learning for
after all he was half Egyptian.

When the time came, Hagar was afraid at leaving her
son and going off without him, but she knew Emuel could
be trusted. If she could find none of her kinspeople, Emuel

would let her assist with selling the wares they would take and the larger task of stocking the carts for the return. Emuel took five employees on the journey, three men and the wives of two of them. Two people always stayed with each cart, so that Hagar would never be alone. Emuel assured them that there was little need to fear for bodily safety—the danger was in being parted from one's gold in exchange for gaudy trinkets by shrewd merchants. Hagar kept her gold inside a pouch securely fastened to her under skirt.

Emuel had an uncanny ability to get news from all parts of the earth. Even before they reached Egypt, he had learned that Hagar's mother had died some years ago but one brother was still a servant of the king. She should be able to learn the whereabouts of her two sisters and her cousins, she conjectured. She was not surprised nor upset to hear of her mother's death for Hagar had buried her in her dreams long ago.

Not a lot of memories remained for Hagar as they passed into the land of Egypt and she wondered if faces would be more familiar than places. Sites sparked no recognition and she felt as if she had never been in this place before. She was not even sure that she would recognize her own brother.

They came to the site where the merchants set up their wares and Emuel told her to assist with the carts while he went to get word to her brother of her presence and location. She was to wait for a family member to come to her. On the second day the sister born just after Hagar, along with her son, came asking for the caravan of Emuel. When Hagar heard the voice, she was stilled instantly for it was the voice of their mother. She stood silent for a long moment, holding at arm's length the sister she thought she would never see again. Her face was like Hagar's but there was more beauty. Hagar saw a softness and hoped her sister's life had been more gentle than her own. A flood of joy rampaged through her mind and she thought she should thank Jehovah, but instead she whispered, *"Thank you, mistress Sarah. I would not be here except for you."*

The sister's name was Eura and she proudly presented her son, Makaim. He and Emuel devised a plan of keeping in touch regarding departure date and Hagar set off to visit with her sister and other family. And what a visit it was! She wished over and over that Ishmael could be with her and know all the kin, but otherwise it was a perfect reuniting.

Eura's husband owned a vegetable market and they had a house of their own with four rooms. Like Hagar, she had one son, thus much of the conversation was comparing and praising their offspring. On the second evening with Eura other kin came; there was the other sister and her brother, who was still a servant of the king. And then there was cousin Sula and her daughter Mali. When Hagar met Mali she especially wished Ishmael were there. Mali was strong with a healthful glow. She looked as though she had been at one with the land and that she could bear many sons. Hagar found it hard not to press her for plans in the future, but instead she reviewed for those who had not heard, the story of her life since their childhood together and they compared it with the ideas they had about what was happening to her.

Hagar did tell them of her experiences with the God Yahweh, Jehovah, but stopped short of telling them that God had promised to make of her son a great nation. They did not respond to her account of God speaking to her twice in the wilderness and providing springs of water when heretofore there was no water there.

Hagar had five glorious days with her family, mostly catching up on years of lost conversation. The only place she wished to see was the palace from the outside, which proved to be the only site that held any familiarity to her. She was totally comfortable with her family and the one complaint was that there were too many people everywhere. Sometimes Hagar felt that with so many people about, they would breathe up all the air.

Throughout the visit, Hagar turned the conversation to young cousin Mali to learn as much about her as possible. On the next to last day of the visit, she approached Sula and her husband with the idea of Mali becoming a wife for Ishmael, an idea not accepted with joy, yet not rejected outright. The Egyptians did not wed near kin but then Mali hardly fell into that category. The bride in Egypt had some choice in the selection of a husband and Mali had never even seen Ishmael. Hagar did the only thing she knew to do. She described Ishmael to Mali and secured a promise that Mali would take no other man for a year, when Hagar would return, bringing Ishmael with her.

Hagar did not use the gold given her by her son, but instead saved for the intended purpose of being applied to getting needed finery and necessities when he and Mali were wed.

As soon as she returned home and Ishmael came in from the grazing land she intended to tell him. Instead he welcomed her and said at once, *"I have had news. Mistress Sarah is near death."*

CHAPTER TEN

The news Ishmael had heard was true. As Sarah's life was ebbing fast, Abraham had moved his family and his large holdings back to Hebron in the land of Canaan, which accounted for Ishmael getting the news. A seller of spices traveled regularly from Canaan to Edom and had stopped to learn whether Emuel had returned from Egypt.

Abraham was disquieted but did take comfort of his son. The immediate question was a burial place. Abraham had not been able to think of this earlier for he could not bring himself to the point of her death. When word spread of the passing, people came from many miles to comfort Abraham.

He rose to stand by the body of his beloved and first thanked those present for their kindness. Then he added, *"Here I am in a land that is not my birthplace, where I own no land and I have no burial place for my wife. Would one of you descendants of Heth sell me a spot so that I can give my dead a proper burial? And I have promised her that when I die, I will be laid aside her."*

One of the men present, Ephron by name, spoke to say that he had a choice cave suitable for burial and would give it to Abraham without price. Abraham was moved by such generosity and bowed himself in acknowledgement. He expressed his gratitude but insisted on paying the worth of the sepulcher. A price of four hundred pieces of silver was agreed on, thus Sarah was laid to rest in the cave of Ephron at Machpelah, near Mamre.

Abraham was more lonely than he ever thought he would be. He missed Sarah specifically and he missed having a woman in his immediate household. He had been suggesting to Sarah for two whole years that they should begin to seek a wife for Isaac but she would hear none of it. Now was the time.

One afternoon Abraham felt a pain in his chest and wondered if he too was going to die. He lay on his soft mat as he called for his servant Eliezer and made him swear by placing his hand under the thigh of his master that he would not let Isaac marry a girl who was not a Hebrew and would never let him marry one of the girls in the area where they lived. Eliezer took the oath, knowing full well if it came to be, he would hardly be able to make demands of Isaac. But then he knew Isaac was most unlikely to assert his rights. Next Abraham asked his servant to make the long trip back to Haran, the land he had left, to find a wife for Isaac from their own kin. Eliezer was not afraid of the long journey into a strange land but he feared that no suitable wife could be found once he got there. And if one should perchance be found, would she be willing to leave her home and go with a stranger to a far land to marry a man she had never seen? He expressed his fears to Abraham, who responded, "*My request is that you go. If you fail, then you are released from this oath, only do not let Isaac go to Haran at any time. He must remain here for this is the land God has promised him.*

May Jehovah God send his angel with you to guide you to the chosen wife for my son."

Isaac was told of the plan and was well pleased with the undertaking. He had sensed the displeasure of his parents whenever he had talked with any of the maidens he had met and thus wondered what his future was to be. He knew his father would depend on Jehovah to give him instructions.

So Eliezer took ten camels, provender and gifts for the future wife and set off for Haran in Mesopotania to seek the family of Nahor. All the days of the long journey he prayed not for his own safety but for the success of his mission.

At long last he reached the city of Nahor near the end of the day. He came to a well of water outside the city and Eliezer was suddenly dispirited, wondering how he would know which woman to approach for many were coming already to draw water. He did the only thing he knew to do, he prayed to Jehovah thus, *"I stand here by this well of water and the daughters of the men of the city come out to draw water. O Lord God of my master Abraham, let it come to pass that the damsel to whom I shall say, "Let down thy pitcher that I may drink' and she reply 'drink and I will give thy camels drink also' let the same be the one thou hast appointed for thy servant Isaac. Thereby I will know that thou hast shown kindness to my master."*

Before Eliezer had spoken the last words of the prayer to Jehovah, a damsel very fair to behold passed near him. Had he not just talked to God, he would have lacked the courage to speak to her because she was more than any man could desire. So Eliezer quickly approached her and said, *"Let me, I pray thee, drink from thy pitcher."*

"Yes, gladly my Lord," the maiden replied, lowering the pitcher from her shoulder. *"And I will gladly draw for your camels."* Eliezer watched as she brought pitcher after pitcher

of water for the camels. Then he asked her name. She replied, *"I am Rebekah, the daughter of Bethel, the son of Milcah whose husband Nahor is dead."* Eliezer asked whether there was room in her household for him to lodge and she answered that there was room. Then he gave her an earring of pure gold and broad bracelets of gold for each arm. Rebekah left running towards home, leaving Eliezer thanking his God for answered prayer.

As soon as Rebekah told the others what had happened and showed them the gold ornaments, her brother Laban ran to the well to beseech the stranger to be their guest. All the family hastened to make him welcome and to attend the camels and the men who drove them. The women added to the supper they had prepared already and gave Eliezer the seat of honor. He requested that he be able to relate his mission before the meal, saying his soul was too full to take on food until it was emptied of the purpose of the coming.

They sat numbed as he told them he was an emissary from their relative Abraham. Then he told of how Jehovah had given Abraham great wealth, even enumerating the wealth. He continued of Sarah's desire for a son and how God had dealt with her in her old age. When he told of Sarah's death, Milcah interrupted to relate the circumstances of Sarah's mother's death and burial. Eliezer then approached the purpose of his mission, stressing his prayer at the well and how Rebekah's actions fit the prayer request completely.

When Eliezer had talked long, then Laban and Bethel conferred and responded, *"We cannot say yeah or nay to your request for it is of God."* Bethel said that Rebekah was a virgin and that she was an obedient daughter and always there seemed to be some special plan Yahweh had for her. Leban added, *"Here is my sister, take her with our blessings."*

Eliezer continued to ignore the food that had been set before him as he went to his knees to praise God for the success of his mission. Then he sent word to the men in charge of the camels and they brought the gifts of gold and silver and fine raiment for the wife-to-be of Isaac and for her father Bethel and her brother Leban and the others of the family. There was so much gladness that little of the food was eaten.

Early the next morning Eliezer said, *"Send me on my way. I must return in joy to my master."*

"I pray thee do not be in haste," Leban begged.

"Nay, I must not haste to send away my daughter. Pray tarry a week or ten days or so. Let me become accustomed to the thought of her leaving," insisted Bethel.

When Eliezer pushed them, they suggested that they should let Rebekah herself make the decision. She was called and they asked her, *"Are you willing to go with this man?"*

"Yes, I am ready to go," she answered.

That settled the matter so they loaded all her personal belongings and the belongings of her nursemaid since childhood onto the backs of the camels in readiness of the long journey.

All the family accompanied Eliezer and his men and Rebekah and her maid as far as the city well, where their water pitchers were filled and farewells were expressed. Rebekah kissed all the family and as she departed they called out, *"May our God bless you and make you the mother of multitudes and may you overcome every enemy."*

They traveled many days and Eliezer was very solicitous of Rebekah. Often he rode near enough to her to engage in conversation so that by the time they neared Canaan Rebekah felt that she already knew the young man who was to become her husband but she became anxious as they neared the place that was to be her home.

"I hope I please Isaac. Do you think I will?" she asked of Eliezer.

"That you will!" was his firm assurance.

Soon she saw someone far away walking alone in a field where sheep had grazed down the green grass. *"Who is that in the distance?"* inquired Rebekah.

Eliezer shaded his eyes with his hands and it took several minutes before he could discern the figure. *"It is my master's son. It is Isaac!"*

Rebekah ordered the camel stopped and asked to alight. She quickly covered her face with her veil as Isaac walked towards them and was met by Eliezer. After a conversation in whispered tones, Eliezer brought Isaac to Rebekah and told her to walk with him to the tent of Abraham. Rebekah was not sure her legs would support her body in order to walk by a man so stately and who more than fulfilled every dream she had ever had for a husband. She could only say a few soft words of greetings, made even softer in tone by the veil. Isaac took her hand and led her to present to his father. When they reached the tent, Rebekah's maid came from behind and turned back the veil. Isaac and his father were both overcome by her beauty. Isaac said, *"You are even fairer than my own mother."*

"If that could be," Abraham added, as memory of taking his own bride swept over him.

Sarah's tent had been prepared for them and as soon as Rebekah had been provided fresh water to drink and to bathe her feet, and personal needs met, she was led to the tent of Sarah and she and Isaac became husband and wife.

CHAPTER ELEVEN

Ishmael stayed near his mother most a whole day as she resumed her tasks after her return from Egypt. As she worked, she recounted the trip and the unfamiliarity of her homeland. She introduced each of her family members in the order she was reunited with them, describing their physical features and emphasizing any similarity to herself or her son. The enthusiasm and rapidity of the accounting lessened none and at the last Hagar mentioned the name of Mali. *"I wish to take her to be your wife."* She almost blurted out.

Ishmael did not appear surprised, nor did he in any way reject the idea. *"Mali,"* he turned the name over in his mind, *"Mali."*

"But she will not have you till she sees you with her own eyes and she likely will want a house. She is not accustomed to tent living nor for having the stars as a ceiling."

Ishmael thought aloud, *"I have already been to the teacher in the village for one lesson. In a few more lessons I will be able to write a greeting to her and send it by Emuel.*

The Egyptians make much of writing, I am told. As for a house, I can make a house. I loathe any structure whose sides cannot be rolled up but I can make a house."

Then Hagar told of the agreement that Mali would not take another man until a year had gone and that she promised to take Ishmael to Egypt at the end of the year so that they could become husband and wife there, if Mali agreed.

"Does Mali worship Yahweh?" Ishmael asked, to Hagar's surprise.

"It is unlikely. I think they did not believe that Jehovah God spoke to me. I did not tell them that you are to become the father of a great nation."

"Do you think Mali will be happy to have many children?" Ishmael asked.

"I am certain she will give me many grandchildren. Yahweh has said!"

And so both of them began to plan and hope for the quick passing of the seasons and to dream of the journey to Egypt. Ishmael was able to send his written greeting to Mali, to be delivered to Hagar's brother at the palace, when Emuel went on his mid-year journey.

Emuel gave both of them gold for the year's wages before they set off with the caravan on the much-anticipated mission. Ishmael took a donkey, as much to impress Mali as to prevent her walking the long distances in the event she was unaccustomed. Ishmael wished he could move faster than the caravan's pace, but otherwise he took pleasure in unfamiliar sites and new kinds of vegetation. He saw a serpent different from any he had seen and followed it as it slithered into the bush. His mother had told him of the Red Sea and he went ahead of the others in anticipation, much as a child might do.

They came to the location where Emuel usually set up

his goods amid many other merchants, and waited for a kinsman. Ishmael was overwhelmed by the noise and the press of the people. He knew at once that if Mali was to become his wife, she would have to be willing to live where he lived. Sheep were not nearly so noisy!

It was Mali's father who came for them, curious to see Ishmael. When he had looked his future son-in-law over carefully, he and Hagar went aside and talked in low tones. Ishmael comforted himself with the observation that if the man didn't look really pleased he did not look displeased. Soon his mother told him that they were ready to go to the house of her sister, where he would be made acquainted with Mali. For the first time, Ishmael became apprehensive. What if she found him unsightly? Or what if she was not to his liking at all? Would he have to give up his freedom to stay inside a house with a surly wife? What if her life's pleasures were not his? What if she cried for Egypt? He lagged more and more behind until her father called back to him, *"Mali is having many fears of meeting you and of the future years."*

At the house they went inside and he noticed there was a chair for everyone; no one sat on the floor. He was motioned to a chair as his eyes darted from stranger to stranger. Then he found the one who must be Mali, the youngest in the room, her face half covered, the other half with a bright red blush. Otherwise, he liked her face. In fact, he liked the blush for he too was ill at ease. All the kin greeted Hagar with warm hugs and kisses, while they visually inspected and evaluated Ishmael. He thought they were looking him over much as he would a ram that he was thinking to purchase. To add to his discomfort, his mother began a sales talk, like the owner of the to-be-sold ram might. *"This is my son, Ishmael, sired by the Hebrew Abraham, who reads and writes Hebrew and Aramaic, but is a man of the fields, skilled in hunting and herding and who desires to take Mali to wife so that he may raise up many sons to become a great nation."* Then she introduced each of those present, ending with Mali. It was an uncomfortable time for both the young people, neither of whom had done more than nod and smile weakly.

Eura, Hagar's sister, finally proposed letting the would-be lovers take a walk outside while the parents talked. Ishmael and Mali hastily excused themselves and were alone together for the first time. Ishmael spoke first, *"I have never been in the company of a maiden alone and I do not know what I should say or do, but I am asking my God to let my mother and your father permit me to take you to wife."*

Mali smiled warmly and replied, *"That is a kind thing to say. I have been in the company of men all my life and none could have behaved more appropriately. I think you were born with the way to treat a woman."*

"I had two mothers," Ishmael said as though to explain, *"one who loved me and one who did not. One used me to gain attention and respect from her husband. The other loved me for myself. I know how to respond to respect as well as disrespect."*

"You speak like a prince but your appearance is that of a desert outlaw," Mali told him.

"I am both," Ishmael responded. *"Do you find my appearance unbecoming?"*

"No. I noticed your strong arms and the mixture of two races of people give you a look unlike most other men. I like that."

Pleased at the comment, Ishmael returned the compliment, *"And I like the beauty of you and that you look as though you could sleep under the stars as well as in a house."*

"That I could do. I like animals and the soil and the heavens."

Ishmael cut her off with, *"The heavens! Do you believe our God Yahweh made the heavens. Do you worship the one God?"*

She seemed a bit puzzled at the idea of the God, one God and Ishmael hastened to say, *"When I was near death in the wilderness, Yahweh gave me back my life. My God is important to me, but we will talk of this in the future. I am of the age to take a wife, past the age for many men. If you become my wife, I will be a good husband to you and one thing I promise is that I will never, never, never take another wife nor a concubine. I know what that does."*

"I shall miss my country and do regret to leave my land but visits may be possible, no?"

Ishmael thought aloud, *"My father and grandfather left their land and you will be doing likewise. I have heard of late that my father took a wife for his other son out of the homeland he left, and my mother is taking a wife for me out of the homeland she left."*

"We talk as though the decision has been made. Perhaps we should wait for their say," Mali commented.

"I shall be ready to have you to wife tomorrow or the next day, if you wish," Ishmael said.

"And I shall be ready to be your wife, if you wish."

Mali's father came searching for them to return to the family to hear the decision. As the pair reached the doorway, they paused and each gazed into the eyes of the other. Then he took her hand and was warmed by their first touch. He led her inside to hear the verdict of their future.

Her father spoke first, *"Ishmael, we are willing for Mali to be your wife under certain conditions. You must treat her kindly and with respect and you must take no other wife. We do not wish to let our daughter go never to see her again so we desire a covenant that you bring her back to us to greet us at times in the future as the gods may provide."*

Hagar gave Ishmael a nod to respond and he answered, *"As touching the first two requirements, you need have no worry. I have already made these two promises to Mali. As for returning her, I can give assurance of that. In fact, I may become a merchant trader also, so there will be frequent opportunity."*

Hagar added, *"And I shall also be on some of those journeys. My son will be a good husband and I shall be a good mother-in-law and I am going to be an excellent help with the children."* The remark brought laughter, as it was intended to do.

The next evening was set as the time for the marriage and the journey home was scheduled the following day. The marriage day was busy for everyone but Ishmael. His only assignment was an hour after mid-day to talk with Arim, Mali's father, and to receive instructions two hours before the wedding. He wondered all morning what to expect and approached the meeting with Arim with some dread. Her father began, *"It is not easy for a father to see his daughter leave his house. For me, it is twice difficult for I see my daughter leave both house and homeland. I shall not be able to hold her children on my knee or teach them to fish the Nile or yet take them on journeys to Memphis. At least not often. If my daughter should be in need, I shall not be able to aid her. Her mother and I can only trust that you will be a good husband to our daughter."*

"I will. I promise that," Ishmael eagerly insisted.

"We have concern that your father turned your mother out when she displeased him. How shall you know how good husbands treat their wives? I do not wish my daughter turned out if she does not please you. In Egypt, a man has no right to do such. A woman is equal to a man and my daughter has grown up expecting proper treatment."

Ishmael responded quickly, *"Remember that it was my*

mother who was turned out. There is no way in which she would ever let this happen to anyone else. I am a man of the fields and there may be many nights when I will not be able to get home to my wife but I will see that she is cared for always, as well as respected and loved. My God has helped me thus far and He will help me be a good father to our daughters and sons. My father is a great man and he taught me many valuable lessons as a child. I still respect him for that."

"I have to trust you with my daughter," Arim replied. *"You have not had a father to talk with you on the way with women and I shall not presume to act your father, but be gentle with her, when you sleep with her, sleep gently."*

"I shall. I may be a man of the wild but I am also gentle and tender. I have often mended the broken wings of birds or rescued lost, frightened sheep. I shall be very gentle with my wife and children. It is my nature. But may I ask you what is expected when the marriage takes place today? Are customs different in Egypt?"

The answer came cautiously, *"I do not know your customs so I may not answer aright. At the appointed hour, Mali will be dressed in white robes with a white veil covering her face. The men of our family will accompany you and Hagar from the house of Kamir and Eura to our home. When you arrive, you will be welcomed inside by me and my wife. Mali will then enter the room, led in by some of her friends who will be singing wedding songs. I have forgotten which songs, and I will then take her by the hand and lead her to you. I will ask if you will honor and love her. You will so promise and I will put her hand into yours. If you have a wedding gift, you give it to her then. Her attendants will turn her veil and you shall kiss her cheek. Then the two of you will be led out and her friends will toss flowers as you go out the door. Her female friends, and after them the kinspeople and others, will follow you to the house of your aunt Eura where a feast will await. All will feed more than plentifully and then with solemnity and joy her mother and I and your mother will escort you to the room, which has been prepared as the bridal chamber. We will join in good wishes. The two of you will acknowledge and thank us and after a bit you will close the door and all will leave the two of you alone. 'Do not hasten to close the door is the one piece of advice I shall give you. Your mother and your aunt will instruct you again, of that I can be sure."*

"Thank you for telling me all this. My mother has purchased a wedding garment for me and she has made sure I am ready to receive instructions two hours before the wedding. She thinks I will not be at ease, but I shall. I will enjoy whatever pleases Mali. And I am glad to have some sense of what is expected."

Ishmael made it a point to get his mother alone before the final instructions were to be given and anguished to her, *"I do not have a wedding gift! I should have a wedding gift! Mali deserves a gift. My father Abraham is rich and I am so poor that I cannot buy a wedding gift for my wife!"*

"How can I comfort you! What can I tell you? I did not know until it was too late. All the gold we had was spent wisely. You could not stand beside Mali in a shepherd's robe. This is a happy day for you. Let us just thank God for all the blessing He has given," she said, reaching up to embrace him.

The instructions to the bridegroom were given, in great detail by Sula, the mother of the bride. When she said, *"If you have a gift for the bride, this is when it is given,"* he made no response. He wondered when the actual time came whether he should say aloud that he had no gift, whether to whisper to Mali that she was marrying a poor man, or whether to tell her father in advance that he had nothing. He was still pondering which would be the least embarrassing to Mali when the first guests began to gather at Eura's home. His cousin, Makim, greeted each and presented them to Ishmael, if he had not already met them and thoughtfully called the name of those he had met. Ishmael was in the house when Makim announced that the trader Emuel was outside and desired a private audience with the bridegroom. Seeing Emuel was a surprise but his mission was a shock. *"I have come to attend the marriage,"* he said. *"I have never paid you the full wage you deserve and am giving you this to offset that lack."* He pressed into Ishmael's hand an exquisite silver bracelet set with gemstones and said with a sly smile, *"I was not sure you had a gift for your bride. That is a custom in Egypt, I learned."* Ishmael grabbed him in a bear hug and could hardly let him go. There was a knock on the door and Ishmael said to Emuel, *"Tell my mother,"* as Makim announced that Ishmael needed to go to the head of the processional.

The wedding event was the most elaborate occasion Ishmael had ever witnessed. The march to the home of the bride was festive as the groom's men cheered and extolled him. Arim and Sula's house was decorated with flowers and branches and they welcomed the groom with great warmth. Ishmael had been told what to expect but he was not prepared for the pomp and grandeur. To him the best part was seeing the expression of surprise and delight on Mali's face when he presented the wedding gift. He stole a quick glance towards his mother, but her eyes were turned heavenward.

CHAPTER TWELVE

Back in Hebron in the land of Canaan, Isaac was comforted of his mother's death by his bride Rebekah. But the aged Abraham found no comfort for his grief. That lack of comfort and sense of loss may have been responsible for his decision. Or perhaps the motivation came from seeing the beautiful Rebekah sporting with her husband. Or may be it was just the way of a man, but Abraham decided to take a wife unto himself. It had been important that his son not marry a woman who worshipped idols but Abraham knew it would be senseless to seek a wife from his kin in Haran and began to look around him for a helpmate. In the city he saw a woman named Keturah, who was not young nor yet old, and who had appeal for him. He approached her and inquired whether she had a husband. He was pleased when she let him know that she had neither husband nor father and Abraham told her he was seeking the one who could give him permission to take her to wife. She told him where to find her oldest brother and the next day Abraham took Keturah to wife.

Isaac and Rebekah removed a distance from Abraham in order to oversee their extensive holdings of sheep and cattle and goats. Too, Keturah was promptly with child, to the resentment of Rebekah, for she had not conceived.

Before Keturah birthed Zimran, Abraham took a concubine and established her in a tent near his own. Then before the birth of Jakshan to Keturah, Abraham took a second concubine and established her near the tent of the first. Abraham liked having sons and Keturah gave him a total of six. The concubines also contributed to his line of descendants.

As the children grew up they, and the passing of time, made Abraham feel the weight of years on his shoulder. He thought of God's promise to make of him a mighty nation and with all the children, this promise was more realistic in his mind. There was also the part of the promise that through Abraham's descendants the world would be blessed. It was his understanding that the blessing was to come through the firstborn son and he attached great store to the promise. He had seen the conflict between the sons of Keturah and the sons of the concubines and set to imagining what would result if these sons should war against Isaac after he was gone. Abraham thought about Ishmael, actually the firstborn, but recalled that God had promised to provide for him. Sarah had told Abraham time and time over that Isaac must be his only heir. He remembered that Jehovah God had sanctioned sending away Ishmael so that he would not inherit with Isaac and Abraham reached a decision to send away all the present heirs who might be a threat to Isaac. He set a date and called the mothers of his children together and told them his remaining days on earth were few. He praised them for the strong children they had borne and spoke honestly of his belief that God desired only Isaac to be his heir upon his death. He settled a goodly sum on the children of the concubines and a greater amount on the six sons and the daughters of Keturah, all to be received upon their departure. Abraham recommended that they go to the east country but set no date by which they must absent themselves and their children. He also allowed them to take a tent and personal effects desired. He worried not what they would do, for after all many of these children were older than Ishmael when he was sent away with his mother and they carried with them only bread and water.

CHAPTER THIRTEEN

Times were changing. There were far more traders and they brought and carried news from around the world. In fact, Emuel had carried word to Egypt that Mali was with child well before time for the child to be born. And Ishmael had received word that Abraham had sent away all the children of his old age in anticipation of the end of his earthly days. Ishmael was able to send a message to his brother Isaac that he would like to be with their father during his last days and he also let Isaac know that he had no quarrel with him.

Word soon came back through the spice merchant that it appeared Abraham's days were few indeed and that Ishmael was welcome to come. In fact, Abraham was requesting to see him. Ishmael went at once to Mali to discuss with her his desire to go to his dying father, a need she supported completely. Next he went to let his mother know of his plan. Her only request was that should he be offered silver or gold, it be refused. It was so important to Abraham and mistress Sarah that Isaac be the sole heir, she wanted no part of what might be considered his alone. God had provided well for her son and she wished nothing else. Next Ishmael went to Emuel, who agreed that if there should be a need he would intervene with the herdsmen and would be of any needed help to Ishmael's women. With that he set out on the long journey to Canaan but he got there too late. His father had wanted to hold on until he arrived but it was not to be. Abraham died some six hours before his firstborn arrived. Isaac was deeply grieved and was glad to have his brother to help in some of the decision making and planning.

There was much stirring and mourning and visitors for Abraham was revered in the kingdom. Some came because they had heard of the beauty of the son's wife and this would likely be an only opportunity to see her. Some came out of fear of the God Abraham worshipped, but most came as evidence of respect for the man Abraham. Ishmael was struck by the depth of the grief of Eliezer, his father's faithful servant of long years. Eliezer, himself infirm in body, clung to Ishmael and wept, *"There was no comfort left in life until today when I see Jehovah God has graciously answered prayers of many years. My master's firstborn son lives! And your mother?"*

Ishmael found Isaac only too glad to relegate many of the tasks of greeting visitors and deciding how the affairs of death were to be conducted. They arranged for a processional of mourners from Abraham's tent to the cave of Mechpelah near Mamre. His two sons chose to bear his body to the burial site and Abraham was laid to rest by the side of his beloved Sarah.

Ishmael recognized that his grief did not compare with that of his brother and he realized his words were not words of comfort but he said, *"Would that our father's death had been in Egypt for there the dead are embalmed and their bodies preserved for years to come."*

Isaac's response was, *"I have heard much of the skill of the Egyptians. I shall not have my father's body but I shall have a sense of his presence with me always."*

The day after the burial, Isaac, Rebekah and Ishmael sat together to review what they knew of their mutual history. At the end of their morning together and mourning together, each decided that they had much for which to praise Jehovah God and that looking back they might have done some things differently from their ancestors.

Isaac did offer to share in their father's wealth, an offer Ishmael promptly declined.

And yes, Ishmael did think his brother's wife of great beauty but he would not exchange her for his own Mali. Rebekah was childless and Mali was already great with their second son. He wondered if Rebekah desired a child and, if so, whether that desire was nearly as consuming as that of Mistress Sarah back then.

Ishmael felt a great ambivalence on leaving his brother. This was the life to which he was born; yet it was a life that would not have fit him. He wondered if he would have been different had he not been cast out, but instead stayed in his father's household. What would the daily living of Mistress Sarah's rejection have done to him? Now he could smile at the idea of having two mothers and of literally having been cast out by the rich one. His own mother had always told him that their God had promised to be a father to him. Ishmael was glad to get back to the wilds where he was at home. A man needed his time alone! A man needed to feel one with his father! He might not see his brother again, and he might enjoy being alone but deep inside, he longed to embrace his son and to hold his wife in his arms again. He was ready to go home!

CHAPTER FOURTEEN

Years had past, years that had been good to Hagar. The hard work was left to others and Hagar passed the time musing on the days of her life and thanking Jehovah God for her good fortune of a multiplying family. For her years, she was still strong in mind and body and often said she knew not whether it was a special reward from Yahweh or it came from years of herding so many grandchildren. She was careful to credit both.

Mali had given Ishmael twelve strong sons and two daughters. Now they were all wed and several times each year there was a celebration for another birth. Ishmael had little say in mates for his children for they were merchants or travelers and took themselves wives from many nations and tribes. Yet each did as the father before them, each brought his mate home. Even the daughters' husbands moved near Ishmael, even though they saw him infrequently.

The oldest great grandson had been named Arim Abraham for his great grandfathers. Hagar was the only one who insisted on calling him by both names and of all the grandchildren and great grandchildren, he was her favorite.

He was only of six years, but could read and pridefully relate his history of being Hyksos and Hebrew. On this summer's eve, he sat near Hagar and asked again about the king who gave her away and how mistress Sarah turned her and his grandfather out to die. Hagar said, as always, *"But let's not be angry at them. What they did may not have been good but had it not happened, I would have never known you."*

"No," young Arim Abraham would reply, *"Because I would not have been born."*

Hagar would go on, *"And I would have never had twelve grandsons."*

Then Arim Abraham would want to hear of how Father Abraham lived in a tent instead of a castle like he and all his cousins lived in. Today he added, *"But mistress Sarah died and father Abraham died and you didn't die yet."*

Tenderly he traced the deep wrinkles of her face and held her thin leathery hands, saying, *"But you may die soon for your face is very old and your skin is too big for your arms and your hair is all white."*

"I will die when Yahweh is ready and you will remember how I told you of Yahweh, sometimes I call Him Jehovah God, and you will obey him."

"But uncle Kedar and uncle Nephish and uncle Kedemare and aunt Mahalath do not think Yahweh is the only God."

"I know," Hagar responded, *"and that makes me very sad."*

"Great grandmother, you have had many things in your life to make you sad. I wish a lot of sad things could have been gladder."

Hagar held the lad close as she mused aloud. *"No, there is nothing in the past I would change. I see now from the long look, and joy grew from every sorrow. It was all for a purpose. I wouldn't change the past and there is only one thing I would change about the present."* Immediately Arim Abraham asked what that was. *"My grandsons are different from one another,"* she said. *"You do not look like your cousins. You have your great grandfather's strong, handsome features. Your brother looks like your mother's family. I do not wish to change any of you but I wish I could change the fact that my children act-out their differences. Your uncles disagree about everything. They argue about Jehovah God and even those who worship him displease him the way they act. They argue about who is richest. They argue over who should be ruler. I wonder if Isaac's family is like mine. I bear your Uncle Isaac no ill will and want you to always remember that his children are your blood cousins. Until we can learn how to live as family there can be no peace in our hearts or minds. Be a peacemaker, little Arim Abraham. That is the most important thing you could ever be. A peacemaker. Your great grandfather Ishmael and his brother Isaac lived in peace with each other. Why c-a-."* Here her voice faltered and her breath came in gasps, weaker and weaker. Startled, the child looked into her eyes to see them roll back in their sockets, as she clutched her chest and slumped forward. He ran calling for his father and as the family rushed to the still body the women began to scream hysterically. His father's eyes filled with tears but Arim Abraham did not cry. He merely looked up at his father and said, *"Father, she wanted us all to live together in peace."*